Resisting the Rancher

Resisting the Rancher

A Hills of Texas Romance

Kadie Scott

TULE
PUBLISHING

Resisting the Rancher
Copyright © 2018 Kadie Scott
Tule Publishing First Printing, May 2018

The Tule Publishing Group, LLC

ALL RIGHTS RESERVED

First Publication by Tule Publishing Group 2018

No part of this book may be used or reproduced in any manner whatsoever without written permission except in the case of brief quotations embodied in critical articles and reviews.

This is a work of fiction. Names, characters, places, and incidents are products of the author's imagination or are used fictitiously. Any resemblance to actual events, locales, organizations, or persons, living or dead, is entirely coincidental.

ISBN: 978-1-949068-42-9

Dedication

To Michelle, Karen, & Patricia
for the fantastic info on rodeos!

Chapter One

WILLIAMS HILL DRAGGED his hand over his face as he sat in his truck at a stoplight in Estes Park, Colorado. After two straight days of driving up from Texas, he was ready to reach his destination of the rodeo grounds in the small Rocky Mountain town. Flexing his shoulders to work out the kinks, he happened to glance over at the vehicle stopped next to him.

Everything in him froze… then released in a pent-up laugh.

The woman driving a shiny new black Ford truck was gorgeous with high cheekbones and pouty lips. Her long hair was pulled back in a ponytail, so he couldn't quite make out the color, but her appearance wasn't what had made him laugh.

She was clearly enjoying a favorite song—singing and dancing for all she was worth, without a care in the world for who might be watching. He chuckled again as she did a little shoulder shimmy. Adorable was the word that struck him, and he was strangely affected, an instant attraction coiling inside in a way that surprised him.

He wasn't an instant attraction kind of guy.

Suddenly, she glanced toward him and stilled as she discovered her audience. Her eyes went wide and she sent him a sheepish grin. He smiled back and pretended to tip an imaginary hat. However, instead of another smile, she went cold on him, eyes hardening, lips thinning. She whipped her head around to face forward, her chin in the air, and didn't glance his way again. She definitely didn't start singing again. Not that she would have had much time, because the light changed a second later.

She was quick to hit the gas, faster on the draw than Will, who was still blinking at her abrupt about-face. He almost expected her windows to frost with the drop in temperature in there. A flash of bright pink on her back window caught his attention as she drove ahead of him. For the second time in a handful of minutes, Will chuckled. The sparkly sticker on the back of her truck read *Silly Boys, Trucks are for Girls*. Lips tipped in amusement, he shook his head.

At the next light, she went straight when he turned, which meant she probably wasn't there for the rodeo. He gave a mental shrug. Wouldn't be seeing her again. Probably for the best, since he was here to work.

Instead, he concentrated on where he was headed as he pulled into the rodeo grounds, his beat-up Chevy truck kicking up dust along the gravel road. It had been a long drive from where he'd stayed in Amarillo the night before. Most of the trip had been over the flat open plains of

Oklahoma and Eastern Colorado. Browns, yellows, and greens had flashed by in a blur of pavement in front and fields of wheat or corn or cotton to the sides.

Will didn't mind driving alone with only Garth Brooks and other old-school country music to keep him company. He liked his own company fine.

He parked, hopped out, and took a deep breath of the pine-scented mountain air. This was the second year he'd provided stock for the Rooftop Rodeo. In the past, he'd gone straight to Cheyenne Frontier Days—one of the bigger rodeos on any of the circuits. He'd been pleased this year to get an invite for several bulls and horses as well as calves at that event. It had worked out in his favor that the Estes rodeo had wanted most of the same stock.

The setting, a mountain town close to the entrance of Rocky Mountain National Park, couldn't be more different form his hometown of La Colinas, Texas. Granite peaks towered above the valley on all sides, creating a cathedral-like effect. The rodeo grounds were located along the main road. He'd driven up via a winding two-lane canyon road and passing the lake. Further down, past the rodeo grounds, was the downtown, filled with quaint shops situated along a walking path that followed the Thompson River.

He'd made decent time, enough to complete the check-in with the rodeo staff before his hands, Chris and Jordan, arrived with the trailers and stock.

He didn't think about the girl in the truck again as they

went through the motions of getting their animals settled before heading over to the Columbine Inn where they'd be staying for the week.

"WHY THE HELL did I smile at that cowboy in the truck?"

Rusty Walker grumbled at herself as she made her way through town, hanging a left before reaching the downtown and following the winding road up to Mary's Lake Lodge where she was meeting a friend for dinner.

"Even if he did have amazing blue eyes."

It had been as plain as the slightly crooked nose on his way-too-handsome face that he was a rodeo cowboy. A Chevy truck that had seen better days, white button-down shirt rolled up at the sleeves, and the tip of his imaginary hat, the real one of which was probably sitting on the seat beside him, had all been a dead giveaway. She rolled her eyes at the mental image, determined not to find his amused grin charming or acknowledge how much she'd noticed on such a short appraisal.

"Not gonna happen, buster."

Rusty *never* associated with rodeo cowboys when she could avoid it.

She'd been raised by one of the toughest rodeo stock providers in the business, and had been around the rodeo and cowboys her entire life. Her father would be less than impressed if she ever brought one home. She could hear him now… "Those buckle boys are about as useless as a screen door on a submarine."

The irony that the men he held such disdain for were essential to his thriving business was not lost on Rusty, but Garrett Walker had his own opinions, and no one, certainly not his daughter, was going to change those for him.

Rusty parked, grabbed her purse, and headed up the wooden steps up to the lobby of the hotel. Mary's Lake Lodge was a huge log structure which stretched along the side of a mountain into a hotel and a series of condos and cabins. All stained dark brown with white trim, giving it a rustic mountain charm she loved, it had a restaurant that boasted excellent food, and an even better view out over Mary's Lake and beyond over parts of Estes Park.

Only half-paying attention to where she was walking, Rusty's mind remained stubbornly on the man in the truck. Her father wasn't her only reason for avoiding the type. She'd learned from painful personal experience that if she wanted a guy who would work side-by-side with her throughout the year, a rodeo cowboy was not her best bet. And if she wanted a man who was in it for her, and not for her connections to her dad, that eliminated everyone else in the business.

Even if the guy in the truck did have the bluest eyes she'd ever seen. Or the sexiest cleft in his chin.

"Nope. Definitely *not* interested."

Why was she even still thinking about this?

Her phone rang, interrupting her dumb internal thought process, but she scrunched up her nose when she read the name on the screen. Apparently one day of peace wasn't even possible.

Looking heavenward for any guidance that might be forthcoming, she answered. "Rusty Walker."

"I expected you to be with the hands," came the gravel-voiced condemnation.

No hello. No questions about her trip. Rusty took a deep breath even as she clutched the phone a tad tighter. "Hi, Daddy."

Deliberately, she put sugar in those words, then grinned. He hated it when she called him Daddy, let alone made it sound sweet.

He didn't even pause. "I asked you a question, young lady."

"I'm sure Travis or Dave have already reported in." The hands were her father's own private snitch network. "The stock is settled and we're all checked in at the hotel. No problems on the drive."

"I already heard that from them."

"Oh." She pretended to misunderstand. "It's nice of you to check on me." She spotted her friend across the parking lot and waved. "I have to go, Daddy. I'm meeting my friend Maggie for dinner, and she's here now. Hugs and kisses."

Rusty snapped the phone closed before he could say any

more. She knew perfectly well he didn't give two hoots about her trip. He'd been calling to make sure she wasn't doing anything to embarrass the Walker name. Like she ever had.

"Howdy, stranger!"

Rusty put her father out of her mind and grinned as she turned toward the sound of her friend Maggie's voice. "Hey!"

The two girls embraced before stepping up to the hostess station to put their names on the list for the restaurant. Maggie was a fellow barrel racer. They'd met two years earlier at the Cody Stampede in Wyoming and had become fast friends, keeping in touch via social media. Unfortunately, thanks to schedules and distance, they didn't meet often. Maggie rode for fun only, and consequently didn't get to a ton of events, and only local. Rusty raced only at the events where her father had stock competing. Granted, that was most of the Mountain States, Prairie, and Badlands circuits. But her racing wasn't about the points for her, it was about training horses for her clients, getting the animals experience, or selling a horse that hadn't sold yet. A "nice little hobby" according to her father. Officially, she was there to represent the family business and help the hands take care of the animals, not that they let her.

As they were seated, Rusty couldn't help thinking about Mr. Blue Eyes in the dented and dusty truck again. He'd turned off for the rodeo grounds. And the fact she'd noticed irritated the tar out of her. However, his supposed destination meant the chances of her running into him over the next week were decent. This was a smaller rodeo as these things went, not like Cheyenne or Houston where she could avoid him more easily. She hoped he'd got the hint that she wasn't remotely approachable and leave her the hell alone.

If he recognized her at all.

WILL WANDERED AROUND behind the chutes, taking in the scene. Dust kicked up, covering everything with a fine layer of gritty dirt. The scents of horseflesh and leather and sweat filled the air, overpowering the subtle pine this mountain town usually smelled of. Men hung around in groups, some up on the rails, some standing, some sprawled out on the ground, sitting and waiting or even fitting in a quick nap. The sounds of the announcer, the music, and the crowds came in and out between riders. Bronc riding was over for the night, barrel racing was about to start, and following that were the bulls.

And even after all last night and most of today without seeing her, he was still looking for the woman in that truck.

"Williams Hill. What're you doin' here, son?"

Will turned to find Chase Schneider standing there grinning like a fool around a wad of chewing tobacco.

"Chase." He nodded, holding out a hand to shake.

"Didn't expect to see your ugly mug here." Chase spit off

to the side. "I thought Rising Star had all the stock tied up for this one."

Will squinted against the sun, which was dipping below the tops of the mountains. "They needed a few more this year, I guess," was all he said.

As a relatively small operation, and one still getting started up, he had to compete with larger, more established stock contractors for every venue, especially Rising Star Ranch when it came to the Mountain States Circuit, but he'd been both smart and lucky that his stock was performing well. However, shooting off his mouth about luck at this particular venue wouldn't win him any friends, not with the potential deal he was about to try to set up.

"They wanted the Turtle, didn't they?" Chase guessed.

Yertle the Turtle was Will's best performing bull. He named all his bulls after Dr. Seuss characters, a thing that had started as a joke, then became a tradition. "He's doing pretty good this year."

Chase didn't seem to notice he hadn't answered the question. "I'll say. He's been racking up points, I hear."

"Yup. You riding?" Will tried to redirect the conversation.

"I finished my rounds for Tie Down tonight. Did okay." He slapped his hat against his thigh, raising up a small cloud of dust.

Will nodded. "I saw your run. Might be time to retire your horse, buddy."

Chase lifted his eyebrows. "Tonight was his last run. How'd you guess?"

Will wasn't surprised because he'd asked around. His business was rodeo stock, but he was more interested in the horses, and Chase's horse was one of the best on the circuit. "You thinking of putting him to stud?"

"I was thinking on it."

"I'd be willing to make you a deal. Give him to me for stud and I'll provide your next two horses."

Chase cocked his head. "I've heard good things about your stock horses, but do you have any solid rodeo prospects?"

Will tipped his hat back and gave Chase a serious stare. "The horses are what we do best." What he did best. The bulls were part of the business, but horses were his focus.

Chase chewed his chaw, considering Will for a long moment. "I'm down Texas way next month. Maybe I'll make the trip further south to check out what you have."

Will played it cool. Getting one of his horses with a rodeo pro like Chase would be a huge coup. "You think on it and get back to me."

"Will do."

Not wanting to push it more, Will moved on. "When are you up on the bulls?"

"Tomorrow night."

"Who'd you draw?"

Chase spit again. "Blueberry. He's pretty good. One you

can get some points on, but he can have an off trip."

Will didn't know that bull, so he didn't have anything to add. "Good luck."

"Thanks." Chase paused as if waiting for Will to keep going.

Most of the guys liked to spend time hanging out while they waited for their events, but Will wasn't much of a talker and they'd hit all the topics he'd been interested in.

Chase obviously realized that because he suddenly grew more serious. "I'm pulling gates tonight for the bulls. Anything I need to know about your animals?"

Will hooked his thumbs in the back pockets of his jeans. It wasn't unusual to get this question. If a cowboy knew his business, then he knew what questions to ask the contractors about their stock. Will, Chase, and Jordan would be behind the chutes helping with the bulls anyway, but Chase showed his experience as a pro to ask regardless.

"The Turtle blows hard, just get the gate out of his way."

Chase nodded.

"Thing Two tends to stall, so watch out for that."

"Got it. Anything else?"

"Nah. Once-ler, Sam-I-Am, and Grinch are all easy. Nothing to do for them except move."

"Thanks, man. Appreciate it." Chase held out a hand to shake again. "See ya 'round." With a slap on the back, he walked off.

As Chase moved away, Will caught a flash of a familiar

horse being led through the crowd of folks behind the scenes.

Interesting.

Attention snagged, he followed. As he got closer, he could see that he'd been right and the handsome quarter horse with a deep red coat and black mane and tail was Mischief Maker, his sister-in-law's horse. The animal was being led by a woman wearing a light pink button-down shirt with a material that shimmered and caught the light along the seams. Her deep red hair hung in a long braid from under her silverbelly Stetson hat.

Will quickened his steps, trying to catch up.

But as he got closer, the woman stopped and quickly mounted. Will realized she was fixing to run the barrels in the event currently going on. Rather than distract her, he decided to wait until her turn was over, then he'd go have a word.

Moving around to an empty spot along one of the fences, he took a step up, looped his arms over the top rung, and settled in to watch. His sister-in-law, Holly, had told him she had sent her best barrel horse to a rider she thought could do something with him. Holly was an accomplished rider herself, but she was also a large-animal veterinarian servicing all the ranches around their area in the Texas Hill Country.

In addition, she was newly married to his brother, which made her a new mama to Cash's little girl, Sophia. While she had agreed to partner with Will, taking on the barrel racers his operation was training, Holly didn't have time to compete herself. He'd been urging her to find a partner all year.

Maybe this woman was a possibility?

As Will watched, two other women made their runs. This particular venue had a longer barrel racing course, but both women made competitive times with a 17.65 second and 17.60 second runs consecutively. Mischief was going to have to ride hard to place.

He glanced over to see if the horse was almost up. With a jerk, he stood up straighter, trying to get a better look at Mischief's rider who was now facing toward him. He'd only seen the back of her a minute ago, paying more attention to the horse.

"Well, I'll be damned," he muttered. More than mere interest about Mischief stirred.

The announcer's voice came over the loud speakers. "Next up, we have Rusty Walker. Rusty's riding Mischief Maker, owned and trained by Holly Hill out of High Hill Ranch in La Colina, Texas. Rusty has taken over the reins in both training and riding this five-year-old quarter horse. Let's see how she does tonight."

With a barely-there signal, Rusty sent Mischief into a gallop. Will tuned out the commentator, the crowds, everything as he watched horse and rider with a single-minded concentration.

Moving so fast, they were almost a blur, they reached the first barrel. The soft dirt flew up as Mischief bent his body around Rusty's leg, turning tightly around the obstacle, as close as they could get without touching it. They popped up and flew toward the next barrel. A smooth lead change, then they hit the second barrel. Mischief almost appeared to pivot on his inside hind leg, his turn was so precise.

Rusty sat fairly quiet in the saddle, guiding her mount more with her legs than her hands, letting him do the job he'd been trained for. She spurred him on toward the third barrel, around it, then rode straight back, Rusty's braid flew out behind her and her legs practically jumped off the horse's sides as she used her heels to urge him to faster speeds. As soon as they were past the line, she reined him in to a sharp stop.

The announcer came on almost immediately. "And she does it, folks. Rusty's time is 17.40, moving her into first place. That was the winning time last year. The other riders are going to have to stretch it to beat her."

The crowd clapped and cheered. With a grin, Rusty waved to them, acknowledging their support for what had been a masterful ride. Holly had made a fantastic choice when she'd picked this woman to ride her horse. No question Rusty Walker knew exactly what she was doing.

She trotted Mischief back through the gate. Will hopped down from the fence and headed her way. Before he caught up to her, she dismounted and lead Mischief back the way she'd come earlier, right toward him.

"Nice ride, Rusty," another dark-haired girl getting ready to make her own run called just as Rusty was drawing up to where Will waited.

She turned and waved. "Thanks, Maggie. Go get 'em."

Rusty was smiling when she turned back around, a genuine smile, and Will could see a pair of deep-set dimples that were downright sexy. Again, that distinct stirring of interest ignited inside him.

"Ma'am?" he called.

Mischief turned his head at the sound of a familiar voice only to be turned back forward by a light tug on the reins.

"Excuse me, ma'am?" Will tried again as he got closer.

Deep brown eyes snapped to his and widened in surprised recognition, at least, he thought that might be recognition. Then the surprise was replaced by a blank wall of cold indifference. The smile vanished, replaced by lips closed tight. She kept walking.

Strangely amused by her attitude toward a total stranger, Will ignored the chill in the summer air, fell in step with her, and held out a hand. "I figured I should introduce myself. I'm—"

"Someone I have absolutely no interest in knowing." She glanced at the hand he still held out, but didn't take it, and didn't stop walking.

Will dropped his arm to his side. "I don't think you understand. I'm—"

"Not getting it. I'm not interested. Quit while you still have some pride, buddy."

Wow. He couldn't remember the last time he'd been

shut down that harshly, and he wasn't even asking her out. All he'd wanted to do was share his relationship to Holly since Rusty was riding her horse.

He held up his hands in surrender. "All right. Great run. Enjoy the rest of the rodeo."

He tipped his hat and stopped walking, letting her move on alone, Mischief following along like the lamb he was, though the horse turned his head to peer at Will a few times in a confused horse kind of way.

Will ignored the animal, his gaze pulled to Rusty's retreating figure and the sway of her hips. Despite her total rejection, desire tightened in his gut, which brought on a frown.

What was wrong with him? What kind of guy found a woman attractive who'd effectively slammed the door in his face before she was even asked? Besides, it wasn't like him to respond so immediately to a pretty woman. Usually, the personality was what attracted him.

A low chuckle had him turning to find Chase not far away. Will raised his eyebrows in question.

"You're not the only one to receive that treatment," Chase commented.

"Yeah?"

They both gazed after Rusty's retreating form.

"Yeah," Chase said. "Her father is Garrett Walker, who's a son of a bitch. Guess that apple didn't fall far from the tree. She's a real ball breaker, that one."

Will cocked his head, still watching as she disappeared around a trailer. While she'd been abrupt to the point of rudeness, he didn't get the feeling that she was a bitch, as Chase implied. Maybe seeing her dancing in her car and the grin she'd initially sent him when discovered had skewed his view.

"I won't take it personal, then," was all he said to the cowboy.

He turned back to the arena, needing to meet up with Chris and Jordan and start thinking about the bulls.

Besides, he doubted he'd see her again after this week, and he was here to work. Not to mention the meeting he had set up with her father for later in the week.

He hadn't missed Chase's casual comment about Garrett Walker, a disposition Will intended to take into consideration, which meant *not* being interested in the daughter. Despite an edge of disappointment lining his mood—one which baffled him anyway—no way would he blow the opportunity.

Hitting on a potential partner's daughter, especially when she'd already blow him off, fell under the category of just plain stupid. Too bad, though.

Chapter Two

"Awesome," Rusty breathed with sarcastic irritation as she read the text on her phone screen.

She was sitting alone at one of the local bars, nursing a whiskey and Coke, and generally ignoring everyone else in there. She had been waiting for Maggie to join her, but apparently that was off now. Some kind of issue with her horse, so Rusty couldn't blame her. Her own animals were like family to her, and if there was ever anything wrong with them, she wouldn't be at a bar. That was for dang sure.

Sucks for me, though.

She wouldn't be in this place if it weren't for Maggie. Rusty'd gone out to eat with Travis and Dave, her father's foreman and top hand who did most of the work with their animals at the smaller events. She was here as a figurehead only, although she intended to change that when she took over the ranch one day.

She'd tried to ditch both men to meet up with Maggie, but they were having none of it. After ditching them last night, they had orders from on high not to let her out of their sight. Despite being twenty-five years old, her father insisted she didn't go to bars or other social events without her "bodyguards." Like she'd ever pick up a random guy in a place like this. Especially a rodeo cowboy.

With a sigh, Rusty pushed the ice in her drink around with the little red straw the bartender had stuck in it. Classic George Straight blared over the speakers loud enough to be heard over the voices of the people packed inside, some trailing outside to the stools that overlooked the river walk. She watched in the reflection of the mirror behind the bar as men and women chatted, flirted, and started the age-old dance that led to hooking up.

For some strange reason, watching others flirt made her think about the guy at the rodeo tonight. The one who'd caught her singing in her truck yesterday. He'd worn a goofy T-shirt that showed a roll of duct tape with the words "My Toolkit" that made her secretly chuckle. No way was she admitting to being hyperaware of the fact he'd watched her ride. She'd caught sight of him before her event.

Rusty made a face like sucking on a sour lemon.

If she was totally honest with herself, the time she and Mischief put up today maybe had a little bit to do with showing off. For him. A touch of guilt stirred in her belly at her behavior afterward. She'd been an out-and-out bitch. No other word for it. Still, better that than encouraging something that would never happen.

Despite her admittedly rude declaration that she wasn't remotely interested, she'd still had to push down an unusual pang of regret at shutting him down. A small part of her wouldn't mind tangling with him. She'd also managed to pick up that his name was Will. One of the other cowboys called it as she'd snuck by later on.

But the fact that she'd been intrigued enough to pay attention had her worried, so she'd crushed the impulse to find out more. She didn't want to know.

"Hey."

Rusty caught a whiff of cigarette smoke hanging around the man who'd taken the stool beside her. She didn't bother to look over, keeping her eyes on her drink hoping he'd get the hint and go away.

No such luck.

He leaned forward and raised his voice. "Hey there, red."

She turned her head and could now see he was swaying slightly. He gave a slow blink, trying to focus, obviously drunk. Great. She didn't acknowledge the guy in any other way, but apparently looking at him was enough encouragement.

"Wanna drink?"

She held up her glass. "I'm good. Thanks."

"My treat when you're done with that."

"I'm leaving when I'm done with this." Maybe sooner at this rate.

He reached out and tugged on her arm. "Now don't be like that."

Rusty sighed. "I'm not interested." She couldn't be clearer than that.

The guy, who was good-looking enough—tall, blond, strong chin, and nice eyes—bristled visibly.

He straightened his back as his eyebrows lowered. "All I did was offer to buy you a drink."

She turned back to the one she already had. "Thanks, but no thanks."

"But—"

"Move along." She waved a hand as though shooing a fly.

He stood suddenly, his stool scraping along the wooden floor with a screech of protest loud enough to be heard over the music and chatter. In the mirror, several heads turned in their direction. Travis and Dave stood up, ready to intervene, but before they could do anything, and even before the jerk could say anything else, let alone touch her, a large hand landed on her shoulder and spun her around in her seat.

"Sorry I'm late, baby," the newcomer murmured.

Rusty only had time to register the new player in the scene was that Will guy with the blue, blue eyes before he leaned forward and kissed her.

She gave a little squeak of protest and he released her lips immediately. The sudden absence of warmth left her feeling slightly bereft, which was crazy since he'd barley brushed his lips across hers.

Before she could process what just happened, he leaned forward and whispered in her ear, "Follow along and we'll get rid of this guy."

Realizing he was now standing between her legs, she hid the shiver sliding down her spine by giving him a tiny nod. He pulled back and smiled down into her eyes. The blue of his eyes, up close like this, was nothing short of startling. The irises were rimmed in black which somehow made the blue even bluer. She could drown in those depths, like falling into the sky, or the deepest of oceans. She had the strangest urge to trace the cleft in his chin.

"Miss me?" he asked, loud enough for the ass on the other stool to hear.

"Of course," she purred.

Some small part of her brain registered that wasn't exactly a lie. She'd spent a ridiculous amount of time thinking about him given their two extremely brief shared moments. They hadn't even been properly introduced or exchanged more than a handful of words.

"Me too," he said as he lowered his lips to hers again.

The moment their lips touched, she was a goner. Sensation rushed through her body, fizzing through her blood with little sparks. She was so attuned to him, she felt every shift, every breath. With a sigh, she lifted her arms, wrapping them around his neck and drawing him in closer. His lips moved over hers in a lazy exploration that left her breathless, and suddenly she was wishing he'd meant it—that he really had missed her.

His tongue darted out, asking for and receiving entrance

to her mouth. The second she granted it, he deepened the kiss, swirling his tongue with hers, nipping at her lips. Rusty gave a little moan. She vaguely registered the jerk behind her swear at them before he sloped off, but she was too wrapped up in Will and didn't give a damn.

She held on to enough of her wits to keep herself from wrapping her legs around him or rubbing against him like a cat in heat. They were in a very public place. The kiss alone was likely to get back to her father—especially with her watch dogs right there. And, although her sense of self-preservation seemed to have abandoned her for the moment, it was still engrained enough to keep her from making a complete fool of herself.

Will finally pulled back, although the action seemed reluctant, like he'd had to make himself stop. She blinked up at him as tried to ignore how he'd let go but put his hands on the bar at her back, caging her in.

Taking a deep breath, she forced sanity to return. *Play it cool, girl.*

She quirked an eyebrow. "I'm not sure if I should thank you… or slap you."

His slow grin tripped her up even as a low chuckle resonated with nerves already on high alert. She liked the sound.

"Whatever you decide to do, might be best if you did it outside." He glanced over his shoulder, presumably for the drunk. "If I walk away now, he'll only come back." He turned back, a question in his eyes.

Rusty wrinkled her nose. "Good point."

She half-turned and, slipping her hand into her bra, where she kept cash and her license when she went out, she tossed some money on the bar. She gave Travis and Dave a little head nod. "Meet you outside," she mouthed.

Then she glanced up at Will, who'd at least stepped back, giving her some space. A long way up. She was petite at a little over five foot, and he towered above her. If she had to guess she'd put his height somewhere around six-three.

She bit back a chuckle as she registered yet another goofy T-shirt. This one read "Always give 100% unless you're donating blood."

He offered her his arm. "May I escort you to your car, ma'am?" he asked in a soft drawl with a gallantry that Southern gentlemen still seemed to display these days.

But sanity was returning to her kiss-addled mind, and she didn't want him to think any of the last few minutes was going to lead anywhere. He must've seen her hesitation because he stepped closer, leaning in to murmur in her ear, "He's still watching."

With a huff of annoyance, she reached out to take Will's arm, not even bothering to look around to check if that was true. Will somehow didn't strike her as the type to lie just to get her alone.

Of course, she'd been wrong before.

They made their way past the few tables between them and the door. The decrease in noise when they finally stepped outside was a blessed relief. A handful of tourists still wandered the street, pausing in front of shop windows, but the crowds had dropped quite a bit since earlier. Without talking about it, she and Will turned to their left to make their way to an alley that would lead back to the parking area. Once they turned down it, Will surprised her by gently letting her arm go.

"Rusty!" Dave's voice brought them both to a halt.

Travis and Dave quickly caught up to them. "What was going on in there?" Travis asked, suspicion lowering his brows.

Rusty opened her mouth to explain, but stopped when Will held up his hands. "I was helping the lady get rid of a drunk."

Before she could say or do anything more, he tipped his Stetson at her. "Ma'am." He gave her babysitters a brief nod then walked off. Strolled more like, as though he hadn't a care in the world.

And, strangely, her annoyance followed him down the street.

How dare he give her the most stirring kiss she'd had in a long, long while, then walk away like it hadn't remotely affected him? Rusty realized exactly how contrary that sounded, even if it was just in her head. With a twitch of her shoulders, she tried to forget about the entire encounter as effectively as he had.

Glancing up she caught Travis's frown. "What?"

she asked.

"Since when do you kiss men in bars?" he demanded.

"Who him?" She stuck her thumb in the direction Will had gone in. "That was nothing. Exactly what he said. He was helping me out of a sticky spot."

Dave nodded, seeming to accept that explanation. "I guess you know him through Holly, huh?"

Now it was Rusty's turn to look confused. "Holly Hill?" she asked. What the hell did the owner of her barrel horse, Mischief Maker, have to do with any of this?

"You know who that is, don't you?"

Rusty shifted on her feet. "We haven't really been introduced."

The two men exchanged a glance. She couldn't tell quite what message passed between them.

"That's Williams Hill."

"Holly's husband?" she screeched.

And he'd just been kissing *her*? That rat bastard.

"Shhh," Dave hissed, a finger at his lips. "No. Her brother-in-law."

"Oh." She deflated like a week-old birthday balloon.

Residual fury swirled with a release of disappointment inside her. The fury she got. Married men weren't her thing, and cheating cowboys on the circuit weren't uncommon. But that swift pang of disappointment, when she'd thought he *was* married, had her concerned. She hadn't had feelings, sexual or otherwise, for a man in ages, and she barely knew the guy. Plus, he was rodeo.

Realization struck. "That must be why he tried to talk to me today. He recognized my horse."

Now she felt like a class A fool, and Rusty didn't like it. A rare blush heated her cheeks, and she was suddenly glad of the dark to hide it from the hands. Rarely was she put so solidly on her back foot like that.

She sighed as she turned and started walking toward her truck, assuming the other two would follow. Now she'd have to find Will tomorrow and apologize for being so rude. Rude twice. She hadn't thanked him or introduced him to her hands tonight.

Damn.

WILL CROSSED THE rodeo grounds in long strides, his boots kicking up the dust, creating a bit of a haze in the otherwise cloudless blue sky. The sun wasn't quite to its zenith, but today was going to be hot. However, he and his crew wouldn't be here much longer, and certainly not when the temperatures hit the forecasted upper-ninety degrees.

They'd made it through the rest of the events, he'd collected his pay, quite happy with the performances of his stock. Two of his bulls—the Turtle and the Once-ler—had earned bonuses which more than paid for the trip. Meanwhile, his broncs had done well too, and he'd talked to several folks about providing stock horses or rodeo horses for them.

Successful trip. Hopefully his time would be rewarded more when he talked with Garrett Walker later today.

He needed to check on his hands, make sure they were ready to roll on out to Cheyenne. Luckily, the drive there was pretty short, so they weren't in a huge rush.

To anyone watching his progress, he hoped he looked his usual steady self, not bothered by anyone around him. In reality, he was scanning the other folks left in the area—like he had been the last few days—looking for a glimpse of deep red hair and chocolate-brown eyes.

He still couldn't believe he'd kissed Rusty in the bar like that.

He'd seen that jerk bothering her for like a millisecond. At first an oddly protective instinct had come over him, like he wanted to land a solid punch on the guy's square chin. But then an unaccustomed sense of mischief had short-circuited his brain. Just like every other moment with the feisty woman had seemed to do. He didn't know what had come over him, going over there to kiss her like that, pretending to be her boyfriend. He didn't react to women like this… ever.

His odd behavior should be enough to have him thrown off-balance right now, but that wasn't what had occupied his thoughts lately. Nope. What had him hotter than jalapeno peppers was that damn kiss—the feel of her in his arms, the hitch in her breathing when he'd taken things deeper, the way he'd gotten lost in the sensation of her mouth under his.

It'd taken a monumental effort to pull back and walk her outside. When her hands showed up, he'd left her abruptly—not because he'd wanted to act all cool and indifferent, but because he'd been so shaken up he'd been worried about making a total ass of himself.

So, he'd left.

He hadn't seen more than a glimpse of her since. Rodeos this size were usually hard places to avoid people, but she'd sure managed it. At least, that was how it seemed to him, and he'd been looking. Not deliberately, but so any flash of recognition had him at attention like a hound on the scent.

No such luck again. He made it to his truck without even a glimpse. She was probably long gone anyway. Although Rising Star Ranch would be at Frontier Days, so maybe...

Will unlocked his car and jerked the tailgate down with a little more force than necessary. *Let it go.*

Hopping up into the truck, he sat on the edge and fiddled with the lock on the box in the bed. He pulled out the large accordion folder he used to store all his paperwork for tax purposes as well as the small safe he used to store the checks and cash he received as payment.

"Hi, Will," a husky female voice murmured behind him.

Will paused, then slowly turned to find Rusty Walker standing behind him. Damn, she was gorgeous. He hadn't imagined that, or the way his body responded, certain parts of him going hot and hard.

Today, she was dressed in simple jeans and a white blouse with puffy capped sleeves and a lace edging. Her hair was loose, flowing in lazy curls down her back. The feminine side of her, at such odds with the tough talking attitude, was perplexingly fascinating. Who was the real Rusty?

She raised her eyebrows when he didn't answer.

Will cleared his throat. "Hi, Rusty."

With more speed than he'd been moving a second ago, he stuffed all the paperwork into what he hoped were the appropriate slots, then dumped the folder and safe inside the lockbox and hopped down. His actions were more about giving himself a second to think and to force his body under control. He leaned a hand against the truck as he peered down at her.

"Can I help you with something?" She'd come to him after all.

Then he blinked as a soft pink color filled her cheeks. She was… blushing? Somehow, he'd never pictured Rusty blushing. But, since his head was already down an inappropriate path, he wondered what she'd look like with that lovely color all over her body?

Jeez, Will. Get your head on straight.

Rusty tipped her chin up at what he could only describe as a stubborn angle. "I wanted to apologize."

Now he felt like a first-rate jerk. She was here to apologize, for what he had no idea, and here he was picturing her in his bed. "That's nice," he said slowly. "For what?"

She hitched a shoulder. "I was… pretty rude to you when you tried to introduce yourself the other day. And I didn't thank you for rescuing me from that drunk at the bar."

Will grinned. He couldn't help himself. "That was my pleasure."

Rusty narrowed her eyes, suspicion shining out at him for a flash, before disappearing and her lips twitched. "Not just yours," she muttered.

Did someone suck all the air out of here? Mountain air was thinner, making it harder to breathe, right?

Will gave her a sideways look. "Ms. Walker, I do believe you're flirting with me."

She laughed, the warmth of the sound washing over him and adding to the tension coiling in his belly. "Don't let it go to your head, Mr. Hill. I must be tired."

He cocked his head, sure she hadn't meant that as a challenge. But still…

"Why don't we put that to the test?" Holy hell. What was it about this woman that had him acting completely out of character?

But the way her eyes widened, then softened, the pink in her cheeks turning pinker, no way was he going to back down now.

Will stepped in close to her, and she didn't back up,

watching him with an expression he couldn't entirely decipher—something between wary and hopeful. He raised a hand to cup her cheek, moving the heavy fall of her hair behind her shoulder. Slowly, giving her enough time to stop him or pull back, he lowered his head until his lips hovered over hers, just out of reach.

But she didn't stop him. With a small hitch in her breath, Rusty went up on tiptoe, closing the distance between them.

Electricity shot through him at the contact. He managed to keep the kisses soft, a give and take that only managed to feed the growing desire flooding his system. With soft strokes, he requested entry, and relished how she opened for him. She tasted of peppermint and summer, a scent of vanilla wrapping around him.

Conscious of their very public location, Will eventually slowed them down. He pulled back to gaze into her deep brown eyes, currently watching him with slumberous desire, reflecting his own need back at him.

"Wow," he murmured.

She took a deep breath, and opened her mouth like she wanted to say something.

"Ruth Francis Walker, what the hell do you think you're doing?" A pissed off male voice hit them like the blast of a shotgun.

At least, that was how Rusty reacted. With a gasp, she jumped back from him.

Whipping her head around, she faced the weathered old cowboy stalking up to them. "Daddy? What are you doing here?"

Daddy? Will took a closer look. Sure enough, the man dressed in black jeans and a black button down with a black Stetson pulled low over his eyes was definitely Garrett Walker.

Damn.

Will resisted the urge to drop his head into his hands. He was meeting this man to discuss a potential partnership. Getting caught making out with his daughter was not the best way to start things off.

Only Garrett wasn't paying him any attention, his focus solely on his daughter with a look that made Will want to step between them, protect her.

"I asked you a question, young lady," Garrett snapped.

Instead of cowering under that gaze, Rusty drew her shoulders back and faced her parent down. "I'm sure Travis and Dave told you about the incident at the bar. This is the man who helped me. I was thanking him."

Garrett didn't even glance over, gaze still trained on his daughter. "Then you send a note. You don't stick your tongue down his throat in the middle of the parking lot where anyone can see. You're a Walker, dammit."

Time to intervene. "Sir—"

Rusty put a hand on his arm, stopping him. He glanced down to find her glaring back at her father, jaw working, and, somehow, he knew she was debating whether or not to keep arguing.

After another second, she sent her father a sweet smile that lacked any warmth, her eyes cold as ice. "You're right, of course. As usual."

Her sudden capitulation only seemed to anger Garrett Walker further. His jaw worked for a solid ten seconds, before he nodded.

Then he turned to Will, his expression completely different, an affable smile deepening the wrinkles at the sides of his mouth.

He held out a hand. "Williams Hill? Glad to meet you."

What the hell just happened?

Will stepped forward and shook the man's hand. "Nice to meet you too, sir."

Rusty glanced between them. "You know Will, Daddy?"

Now Garrett's smile reminded Will of a shark before he chomped down on a helpless victim. "Of course. I'm here to discuss a partnership with him."

The glare Rusty turned on Will was nothing short of venomous. If she'd been a rattler, she would've struck, sinking her fangs deep and pumping him full of liquid poison.

For the second time in almost as many seconds, Will could only shake his head. What the heck was going on here?

"You're trying to partner with my father?" she asked between clenched teeth.

Will raised his eyebrows in question. "Yes," he answered slowly, sensing a trap.

"You asshole," she spat. Then she turned on the heel of her hot pink boots and stomped away.

He glanced at Garrett for guidance, but the old man was staring after his daughter, the light in his eyes both speculative and strangely satisfied.

The beginnings of a headache spiked behind Will's eyes. What had he landed himself in the middle of?

Chapter Three

Rusty didn't bother to wait for her father or the crew. She loaded up Mischief in her trailer, making sure her pissy mood didn't mean a shoddy job taking care of him. Her horses were her babies. Then she hit the road. Sure, she and the hands and her dad would all end up at Frontier Days together eventually. In fact, a larger crew with even more animals would end up there, as it was one of the bigger rodeos in the circuit and Rising Star was one of the major stock contractors for it.

Didn't mean she had to wait for them now.

"Thinks he can get to my dad though me," she muttered as she pulled out of the rodeo grounds onto the road leading back down the canyon to the highway, and then on up to Cheyenne.

"Can't believe I fell for it again," she muttered next, slamming her hand on the wheel for emphasis.

Then she shook out her hand, the fact that it now throbbed only making her more irritated with Will. One would think she would've learned by now that any man who showed interest was actually interested in her father.

She proceeded to have a one-way muttered conversation calling Williams Hill every name under the sun, and throwing in a few choice terms for her father while she was at it, all the way down Thompson Canyon.

Her mood had not eased up any by the time she reached Greeley. Only the ringing of her cell phone cut her off.

She glanced at the name that popped up on her dashboard display and debated answering for a long second. Except she'd promised Holly that now would be a good time to talk.

Finally, she pushed the button on her steering wheel that allowed her to take the call hands-free. "Hi, Holly."

"Ummmm… Is now not a good time? I can call back later."

Dang. Rusty took a deep breath, trying her best to calm down. "No, it's just…" She tightened her grip on the wheel, debating what she should and shouldn't share. "I would love to ring your brother-in-law's neck about now."

Rather than take offence, Holly snorted a laugh. "Is that so? Which one?"

Rusty raised her eyes heavenward. "There are more than two Hill brothers out there." Lord help the women of Texas, because if they looked anything like Will, hearts had to be breaking all over that land.

An amused chuckle came down the line. "Cash has three brothers and a sister."

Will was one of five? As an only child, at least since she'd been eleven, Rusty couldn't begin to picture how that worked. "Well, the one I'd like to bop on the head is Will."

"I figured, since I knew he was up at the Rooftop Rodeo. But why? Of the five of them, he's by far the most laid-back. I couldn't imagine him doing anything—"

"He kissed me. Twice. Before meeting my father to discuss a business deal of some sort."

Silence greeted her declaration. "Oh," Holly finally said.

"Exactly."

"I'm sure Will didn't kiss you to get to your father, if that's what you're thinking. He's not the type."

Rusty wasn't so certain. That sexy grin couldn't be sincere. Still, she wasn't going to argue with his sister-in-law about it.

She gave a little sigh. "I'm sure you're right."

Not that it mattered anyway. Hopefully, she wouldn't see much of him. After all, they hadn't crossed paths before this. Although if her father offered him some sort of deal…

"I'm glad you agree," Holly murmured. "Because otherwise what I'm about to ask might not work."

"Oh?" Dread and curiosity made for an interesting mix as they churned in her stomach.

"I'd like to offer you a job."

"A job?" Hell, she sounded like a freaking parrot. But a job?

Holly didn't seem to pick up on her misgivings at least. "Yes. At High Hill Ranch, working for Will actually." She gave a nervous chuckle.

No flippin' way was that gonna work out. But she managed not to say that out loud. "Shouldn't Will be offering me the job, then?"

Holly chuckled. "It's my job that I'm offering. I promised to partner with him, training barrel racers and other rodeo horses, and I love it. But between my full-time job as a large animal vet and my new family… which is about to get a little bigger…"

Rusty gasped. "You're pregnant?"

A happy giggle drifted through the phone. "Only nine weeks. Please don't tell Will. I want to let him know as it impacts some business decisions. We're going to tell the family when we get them all together."

"Congratulations, sweetie. That's wonderful news! And I won't tell a soul. I promise." Despite her own foul mood, Rusty still smiled. Holly was good people, and deserved the happiness so clear in her voice.

"Thank you. I'm still in shock honestly. This came along a little faster than we'd anticipated. Those Hill men are potent."

Tell me about it. All she'd done was kiss one, and she was still reeling. A fact she now resented.

"Anyway, I was hoping to be able to tell Will I had someone in mind to replace me. Honestly, he needs more help than I can give anyway. That side of the business is growing fast, but so is the rodeo stock side, so he's traveling a lot. He needs someone there full-time."

"I appreciate the offer, Holly—"

"Don't say no!" Holly wailed. "You're the best person I've found. Look at what you've done with Mischief."

Rusty scrunched up her face. Dang, she hated disappointing people. "I'd love to say yes, but I can't. Dad's going to retire someday." Soon, she hoped. "If I'm going to take over Rising Star, I need to…" She paused. She couldn't very well say something like keep proving myself, even though that was the truth.

"I understand," Holly said before Rusty could think of a better way to put it.

"The position does sound right up my alley," Rusty offered. "I'm sorry to have to say no."

"I know. It would've been perfect." But Holly's voice held only chagrin, no condemnation.

"I'd still be happy to take on a horse or two, here and there." That was the best Rusty could offer.

"Thanks. I'll let Will know. Is there anyone you might recommend instead?"

Maybe Maggie? She'd have to ask her friend first though. "Let me think about it and get back to you."

"Sounds good."

Nothing much to say after that, and, following the usual round of pleasantries, Rusty hung up. At least talking to Holly had managed to get her mind off Will and her father, letting her temper cool down a bit.

Holly might think her brother-in-law hung the moon, but the *School of Been There Done That* had taught Rusty if a man had career ambitions in rodeo, she was suddenly considered a ticket to their free ride to success.

Hell, she'd almost married one of the passengers on that crazy train.

Time and experience had shown her Jason hadn't damaged her heart so much as her pride. But once—just once—she wanted a man to love her for herself, and not for her last name. She wasn't likely to get any unconditional love from her father. When her older brother had passed away in a car accident, Garrett Walker suddenly had to contend with the fact that his only heir was not only a woman, but the daughter he already blamed for killing his wife in childbirth.

Probably to her father's annoyance, she'd turned out relatively undamaged and self-reliant. And Rising Star *would* be hers one day, come hell or high water, despite her overbearing, dictatorial father and his old-fashioned opinions.

After that kiss at the bar, she'd almost convinced herself Will might be different from the others. What a dadgum fool she turned out to be. Not as smart as she'd thought, that was obvious.

Flipping on the radio, Rusty did her best to put her father and Williams Hill as far from her mind as possible. A little over an hour later, she was pulling into the rodeo grounds for Frontier Days. She took care of Mischief and got registered, but when she returned to her truck, she stopped in her tracks twenty feet away and considered ditching her vehicle and walking somewhere far, far away for lunch.

Instead, she slowly approached the man waiting for her. "That must've been a fast meeting," she said.

Hard living had taken its toll. Dark skin, leathered by the sun set off pale blue eyes which could turn piercing faster than a stampeding herd. Tall and rail thin, her father might be described as rangy. He kept his face cleanly shaven and hair, more silver than black these days, he wore short and slicked back.

She'd say he looked old, but his eyes were still too keen, and his body still in too good a condition to label him with that description.

Her father shrugged. "I'd already done my research, but I have to—"

"Look a man in the eye," she filled in for him. He said it often enough. "So, it's a done deal? What kind of partnership are you working out?"

With the man who lit me on fire only to be doused by a bucket of cold reality.

"For now, we're discussing transportation and housing for the animals. He's my conduit to more Texas circuit events, while I can help him in the Mountain, Prairie, and Badlands circuits."

She pursed her lips. "Sounds like a win-win, Daddy."

His mouth turned down at the name. He hated that she called him Daddy, which was why she did it. She ignored the frown and passed him up to open the driver-side door to her truck and toss her paperwork on the seat.

When he didn't leave, she raised her eyebrows. "Did you need something from me?"

Her dad put his hands on his still-lean hips and directed his hardened gaze at her from under the brim of his hat, his eyes glittering with a light she didn't quite trust. "You need to know that I'm changing the terms of my will."

Everything inside Rusty came to a screeching halt. He was talking inheritance, which meant the ranch.

Schooling her features to not show her shock, Rusty crossed her arms. "Oh?"

"Rising Star still goes to you…"

A trickle of relief leaked through the tension riding her body, but she didn't let herself breathe easy quite yet. "But?"

"But only if you marry a man I approve of within the next year."

Oh. My. God.

Blood pumped through her so hard, the pounding sounded in her head. Fury and despair warred inside her, and Rusty had no effing clue which to respond to first. Her father resented her, something she had known since she was old enough to understand why he treated her so coldly, when he addressed her at all. That had only gotten worse after Reed died. But she'd *never* imagined he'd do something like this.

By some miracle—and years of experience dealing with

her father—she held onto the words she wanted to scream at him. "And if I don't?" she asked quietly.

"I've determined an appropriate man to inherit in your place. Someone who knows the business."

I know the business.

She wanted to screech. She wanted to cry. Or hit him. Or stomp away. But she wouldn't give him the satisfaction of any of that. Tantrums held no sway with him, and she'd outgrown them a long time ago.

"I see," she said instead, projecting a deadly calm she was far from feeling. "I assume you've already selected a list of appropriate candidates for the role of Mr. Rusty Walker?"

His smile spelled out exactly how much he had her over a barrel. "If you need some suggestions, I have one or two, but, no. You can pick. I just get final approval."

"Uh-huh. Are any of the hands on the suggestion list?" If Dave was one of the ones listed, she might lose her breakfast right here in the parking lot.

That wiped the smile from his face. "No. And if I find out you've been sneaking around with one of them—"

Her snort cut him off. "Yeah, right. Like I'd ever be interested in one of your lackeys."

Then a terrible, awful idea occurred to her. "Is Williams Hill on your short list?"

Please say no, please say no.

But he didn't. Her father shrugged.

Well, shit.

"Was that the deal you were discussing?" She hated that she had to ask, was compelled to ask.

"No."

She believed him. One thing her dad was, was honest. Rusty took a deep breath which she released as a long, audible sigh. "Well, then I guess the ranch will have to go to someone outside of the family."

If her heart wasn't aching in her chest, she would've laughed at the frozen expression of shock on her father's face.

"Excuse me?" he demanded.

She mimicked his shrug from a moment ago. "I may have put up with your blatant hatred that you only have a girl to pass your legacy to, and your iron-fisted control over my life up till now, but I draw the line at this. One day, you'll die, then I'll be stuck with whoever you approved for the rest of mine."

Her father scowled. "That day is coming sooner rather than later, young lady. I need to get my house in order."

For the second time in minutes, shock ricocheted through her like a buckshot pinging around. Did he mean what she thought he meant? "What are you saying?"

His lips flattened. Perhaps he hadn't meant to tell her that. "I've got cancer."

Rusty's chest tightened until she couldn't breathe. He might be a dictatorial, old-fashioned ass, but he was the only family she had left.

"How long?" she asked, hardly able to make her lips

move to form the question.

He spit on the ground. "Couple months. Six at most. It's a brain tumor. Inoperable."

Six months. Or less. And she'd be an orphan. *My father is dying.* Rusty couldn't wrap her head around this new reality.

"So you'd better get a move on. Because I want to leave the ranch with family, but only if I know it'll be run right."

"I would run it right," she said softly.

"After the babies come, you'll have other things to focus on."

A hysterical laugh tried to bubble out of her. He'd just told her he was dying and he was going to take her home away, because she was going to have babies one day.

"I can't, Dad." She shook her head slowly. "I won't."

Garrett Walker's mouth hung open. Maybe the only time she'd ever shocked him speechless.

"I'm sorry you're dying." And she was. More than she'd expected to be, maybe. "And I want Rising Star more than I think you ever realized. But…" She gave her head a shake. "Marriage is too big, too serious, and too long-term for me to rush into it. Even for you. Even for the ranch."

Her father's initial frozen response morphed into a glare that should've left her quaking in her boots, but Rusty was hard-pressed to feel anything but numb.

"I expect you to get your ungrateful ass off my property," he snarled.

As though that would change her mind. She tipped up

her chin. "After the rodeo, I'll be more than happy to oblige."

"With what vehicle?" By the triumph in the smile he aimed her way, he clearly thought he had her there.

"I hate to break it to you, Daddy, but everything I own, including my truck and the clothes on my back, I've paid for with *my* money, funds earned under a company I started and own. I haven't used a cent of your money since I was eighteen years old."

She'd even paid for her college degree. Granted, she was still working off those loans.

He scowled. "That's not possible. You've been accepting an allowance from me for years."

"Why bother arguing with you over it? I let it sit in a bank account, but it's all there. I'll arrange for the bank to transfer it back to you."

The only thing she'd wanted from him was Rising Star Ranch, but that was no longer an option.

By this point, her father's face was turning an interesting shade of eggplant purple. If he wasn't careful, he'd keel over now, before he had a chance to amend the will. Not that she'd wish that on him. The man had six months left to live, and she wished...

Hell, she didn't know what she wished. That she could be there to help him through it. That he could pass in peace, knowing she'd continue to grow and prosper the legacy he left behind. But he wasn't going to let her do either of those things.

"Where do you think you'll go?" he asked.

Her conversation with Holly on the way here suddenly gave her the answer she needed. Fate sure had a sense of humor, not that this situation seemed at all funny.

"That's no longer your concern," she said to her father. "Now, if you'll excuse me, I need to check on Mischief."

Before he could stop her, Rusty walked off.

She made it only far enough away to be sure her father hadn't followed, then Rusty stopped, leaning against a trailer, hands on her knees, as reaction finally set in. Her chest constricted, and she tried to suck air into her lungs.

Oh, my God. Oh, my God. What have I done?

He was dying and she'd walked away. What kind of daughter did that make her? Years of dealing with his dictatorial ways in pursuit of her dream of running the ranch, and she'd walked away. She should've known he'd never just let her have it. Hot tears stung the back of her eyes, but she pressed the palms of her hands into her eyes and refused to let them fall, still painfully aware that she was in a public place.

"Rusty? You okay?"

She closed her eyes at the sound of the deep male voice calling her name from close by.

Will.

Seriously? Had the entire universe decided to dump on her today? "I'm fine," she mumbled.

"You're sure? Because it looks like you're about to vomit, or pass out. Maybe both."

She managed to force herself upright, sucking a sharp breath in through her nose, forcing it into lungs that still didn't want to function. "I said I'm fine."

She went to walk past him, but he snagged her by the elbow, swinging her around to face him. Even now, resenting him almost as much as her father, his touch still warmed her skin, sending a fizz of awareness through her.

"Listen," he said. "I don't know what's going on between you and your dad, but I'm not part of it."

The worst possible thing he could've said to her. A hysterical laugh bubbled out of her. "Whether you like it or not, you're smack in the middle of it."

She jerked her arm out of his grasp. "Have fun dealing with that son of a bitch, because I'm through with trying."

This time, Will let her go, though she could feel his gaze burning a hole in her back as she walked away.

Managing to avoid Will, her father, and the hands, Rusty made her way back to her truck in a roundabout way. She hopped in the cab and pulled out her cell phone, dialing.

A familiar female voice answered.

"Holly?"

"You get to Cheyenne safely?" Holly asked.

Had she picked up on the tension in Rusty's voice?

"Yeah. Um... I think I'm going to take you up on that job offer after all."

Chapter Four

"WHAT DO YOU mean, my hotel reservation got lost?" Will stopped walking in the middle of the concourse, cell phone to his ear, sun beating down on his head, his hat shading his eyes.

"Watch it, buddy," someone grumbled as they passed by, so he moved to the side out of the blazing sun.

The rodeo hadn't started yet, but the place was full of stock contractors, cowboys, and rodeo staff getting everything set up to kick off with the timed slack events before the shows got rolling.

Will put a hand to his head. His day had started off crappy—Rusty and Garrett Walker both having a large hand in that—and apparently the pattern was continuing. Seeing as how the person on the other end of the line was his mother, he was doing his best not to flip out. "Can they un-lose it?"

A deep sigh came down the line. "I'm sorry, honey. They're booked solid. I've checked and every other hotel in town is too. I did manage to find you something…"

Evaline Hill was not the shy type, prone to hold her

tongue, so her hesitation had him a bit worried. "What's the catch?"

"Well… I called around and found Jordan and Chris some space. The Brewers are out there in their camper, and have bunk beds they can spare."

"And me?"

"I've put you up at a B and B in downtown Cheyenne—the Nagle-Warren Mansion."

At least it was a bed and not sleeping in the cab of his truck, which had happened before. "Doesn't sound so bad."

"It a historical Victorian mansion."

Ah. In other words, all dainty antiques and he had a tendency to break dainty stuff. Beautiful, but not exactly designed for a tall cowboy who, as his mother put it, tromped around like a bull in a china shop. "I'm sure it'll be fine, Mom."

As long as he had a place to stay relatively close to the rodeo, he didn't care what it was. He wouldn't be there more than to sleep anyway.

"Good. How'd your meeting with Mr. Walker go?"

Will shook his head, trying to come up with a description. After Rusty left, the conversation had been brief and a bit weird—as though Garrett Walker was distracted—and inconclusive.

"If you're shaking your head, Will, I can't see it."

"Sorry, Mom. Mr. Walker seemed… receptive. But we didn't nail anything down like I hoped."

"You still think he'd be good to work with?"

"He's one of the biggest contractors in the business. So, yeah. I wouldn't call him an easy man though." *And I can't get his daughter out of my dang mind.*

"Hmmmm... Well, you always make the right choices. I'm sure you'll figure it out."

Will had his own doubts about that, but limited his response to a simple, "Thanks."

"Have you talked to Holly yet?"

"No. Is Mariah's foal finally on its way?" Slowly, Will meandered toward the parking lot. He needed to check in to his new accommodations.

"I don't think so. Give Holly a call when you get a sec. She's been trying to get a hold of you."

"Yes, ma'am."

They chatted a little longer. After getting reports on the ranch and his siblings, he hung up with his mother. By that time, he'd reached his truck. His cell phone GPS got him to the B&B, which was a short drive from the rodeo grounds.

The mansion stood on a corner, tall and stately with a wide front porch and a turret. Inside was just as his mother had probably imagined—wood floors, fancy wallpaper, chandeliers, furniture that looked like it'd snap under a butterfly's weight let alone his big frame.

And Rusty Walker.

What were the odds? He'd recognize her head of red hair and her slim body anywhere, not to mention her perfectly rounded behind. To his irritation, his body tightened in a visceral response to her presence. Will clamped down on that hard. She'd already called him an asshole once today. No need for a repeat.

She stood with her back to him and a suitcase at her side as she talked to the lady checking her in. Will didn't say anything, simply stepped up in line behind her and dropped his duffel on the floor.

"I'll be right with you," the lady behind the mahogany desk murmured.

Will tipped his hat, even as he waited for Rusty to turn, but she didn't.

"Here's your key," the check-in lady said to her. "You are in the Sara & Richard Sullivan room on the third floor."

"Thank you." Rusty gathered her suitcase and turned only to stop dead, eyes going wide.

She opened her mouth as if to say something, then closed it again.

"Ms. Walker." Will nodded.

She frowned, but the look she sent him wasn't embarrassed or offended or angry. If he were a betting many, he would've said Rusty was confused. Why? The way they'd parted was pretty darn clear to him, and nothing changed when he saw her in the parking lot earlier.

"Mr. Hill," she finally said.

Then she dragged her suitcase behind her as she headed for the stairs. Will watched her go, still trying to figure out what that look had been about.

"May I help you?" the lady behind the desk asked.

Five minutes later, for the second time that day, Will couldn't believe his luck. Fate seemed determined to throw him in Rusty Walker's path. Or vice versa. He looked at the key in his hand. The key for the only other room on the third floor. With Rusty.

Really?

Still, they might not cross paths. This was a long rodeo, and they might not be scheduled the same nights.

Once up in his room, Will stood, hands on his hips, staring at his accommodations and shook his head. The room was beautiful. In fact, every woman he knew would probably gush over it, but he only hoped he didn't break anything.

He carefully flopped on the bed, then pulled his phone out of his back pocket and dialed. "Hey, Holly. Mom said you were trying to get a hold of me?"

"Yes. Although I was hoping to talk about this in person, but circumstance is throwing that idea out the window."

What now? "That doesn't sound good."

A nervous chuckle reached him. "We'll see." She cleared her throat. "I'll start with the good news."

"Okay…"

"I'm pregnant."

Will jerked up to sitting. "That's wonderful! Of course that's good news, Holly. Cash must be over the moon."

"We both are." He could hear the smile in her voice.

If anyone deserved a large and happy family, Holly and Cash did. Holly'd lost all the adults in her life and had had to let her younger brother and sister go into foster care as she went off to college. She'd thought for years that she wasn't worthy of a family, but Cash had convinced her otherwise.

Meanwhile, Cash had lost his wife in a car accident. Georgia had been Holly's best friend, yet another roadblock to their romance, and Georgia had been leaving Cash for another man that night anyway. He'd been raising their daughter, Sophia on his own ever since.

"So, what's the bad news—" Logic sank in. "Oh."

The fact Cash and Holly had found happiness together was a minor miracle. Will could never wish them ill, even if it did mess with his own plans. He should've seen this coming anyway.

She blew out a long breath. "Yeah. With the practice, and Sophia, and now a new baby on the way... I can't keep working with the horses. I'm sorry, Will."

"I totally understand Holly. Of course your family and your career need to come first."

Immediately, he started spinning the issue through his mind. She'd been handling all the rodeo horses, not just the barrel racers. Will had been traveling so much, he hadn't had time. He ran a weary hand over his face. Seriously? Today could end any time now, because he'd like to write it off. Maybe he'd ask around this week and see if anyone with Holly's skills needed a job.

"That's the other piece of good news. I didn't want to leave you in the lurch. I have someone interested who'd like to take over from me. Even take on more work, coming on full time."

Will perked up. If Holly found someone, then he knew they'd be good—

Wait. No way.

But that odd look Rusty'd sent him downstairs made a helluva lot more sense if his guess was right.

He raised his gaze to the ceiling and cringed. "Don't tell me. Rusty Walker?"

"How'd you guess?"

Will flopped back against the bed, wincing as the delicate contraption groaned a squeaky protest at the abuse. "She's been riding Mischief."

"Oh, duh. Of course."

This was way worse, because no way was he going to stress out his pregnant sister-in-law with his misgivings or trying to find someone to replace her at the ranch. Meanwhile, the stirring of interest, the small spark of something he couldn't quite identify at the thought of having Rusty at the ranch, working with her every day… that was dangerous. Insidious. Rusty's antagonism toward him was not exactly work friendly, and nothing was going to get in his way when it came to the business.

Holly, unaware of his mental churnings, kept going. "Have you seen her ride? She's done even better with him than I expected. She has a great reputation among the barrel riding set, and with her background, can be a real asset in your rodeo side of the business, maybe even freeing you up to pursue the racing side of things like you've wanted to."

Will was too tied up on the Rusty issue to think through the business side. Still, Holly had a point. They'd both set aside Holly's horse, Solario, who showed real speed, as an option neither of them had the time to pursue. But the horse had promise, and if he started right now…

What am I thinking? Rusty was drama, and he was anti-drama. No way could this work.

Maybe hearing the hesitation in his silence, Holly pushed harder. "You should give her a shot, Will. I know she's perfect. And it sounds as though she's ready to start off on her own, away from her father."

Will sighed. "Tell you what. She's here. I'll set up a time to meet with her, watch her work, and go from there."

"Fair enough." Holly's relief was palpable.

Ah, hell. I'm going to have to hire Rusty Walker. No way was he going to risk Holly's health, stressing her out over this.

Still, maybe he could prove to Rusty this week that it wouldn't work. Get her to walk away from the idea. His gut gave a kick of protest at the thought, but Will ignored it. Everything he'd worked so hard to build was too important. Family was the only thing that trumped it.

"I guess I'd better get started," he said.

Holly laughed and told him to have a good rodeo before they hung up. Better to tackle this issue now than put it off. With a groan, Will levered himself off the bed with reluctance and went across the hall to knock on Rusty's door. The only other door on their floor.

No answer.

Huh. Did she have plans? Or had she run off, guessing that if Will didn't know about her job offer, he would soon enough?

He meandered back to his room and lay back down. Slack events didn't start until tomorrow, and she was checked in here, so eventually they'd cross paths.

He flung an arm over his head and stared at the sheer white gauzy thing the B and B had draped over the iron canopy of the bed. Not that he saw it. Snapping brown eyes and glorious red hair just wouldn't get out of his thoughts.

Dang it. The woman was hijacking his brain and now his life without his permission. For the second time, he heaved off the bed, only now he grabbed his phone and keys. Determined to track down one Miss Rusty Walker, he stuffed his hat on his head and made for the stairs, which he had to turn his feet sideways to use since they were skinnier than the length of his booted feet.

An hour later, he tracked her down at the rodeo grounds. She stood at the edge of the Old Frontier Town section of the park talking to another woman with dark curly hair. Maggie, he thought her name was, the same lady from the Rooftop Rodeo in Estes Park. As soon as she saw him,

Rusty's eyes widened. She played it off like she hadn't noticed him walking through the few cowboys milling about and mumbled something to Maggie before turning on her heel and heading the opposite direction toward the parking lot.

Don't you know not to run from a predator, darlin'? Will shook his head and kept after her, tipping his hat at Maggie who stared as he passed by.

Before she could get to her truck, he called out, "Rusty Walker, you're going to have to talk to me sometime. After all, you're trying to get a job working for me."

That stopped her. She stood in the shadows between two campers. He wasn't sure, but her shoulders might have moved in a sigh.

Slowly she turned to face him. "Will. I didn't see you."

Yeah, right.

She shifted on her feet as he finished crossing the distance between them. "I guess you've been talking to Holly?" she asked.

"Yeah." He stopped a few feet away and crossed his arms. "Mind explaining?"

She nibbled at her lower lip. Nervous sign? Or was she trying to decide what to say? Either way, he had to adjust his stance thanks to the inconvenient shaft of desire that one small gesture brought on.

Not good.

"I was going to talk to you when the rodeo was over," she said.

I'll bet. He raised his eyebrows and waited.

Seeing he had no intention of letting her off easy, Rusty tipped up her chin and cleared her throat. "I've decided to leave Rising Star Ranch and… make my own way. Holly's suggestion came at the perfect time. I think I could be a big asset to your horse operation."

Will honestly had no idea which of those statements to address first. He went for the obvious. "You really think you could work with me, given how much you don't like me?"

Though he still had no clue why. Nor did he plan to address the bad taste saying those words out loud left in his mouth.

She raised a single eyebrow, the corner of her mouth tilting up. "You don't have to like someone to work with them," she pointed out.

Ouch. He had to stuff a reluctant laugh back down his throat. She sure didn't pull her punches.

"True," he drawled. "Although, when you live on their property and see that person day in, day out, it does help."

She hitched a shoulder, her only acknowledgement. "The horses and my reputation are what matter to me. Something I thought you'd appreciate as I get the impression it's the same with you?"

He dipped his head.

"Then we'll get along fine. I'll work hard, and I'm damn good."

He believed that. "And if I partner with your father?"

She stepped back, lips flat, looking away. "It's good business for you, so I won't stand in your way. But do your best to leave me out of it."

"If you're training barrel racers or handling any of our other rodeo stock, that might be difficult."

Her shoulders slumped forward slightly. If he hadn't been studying her so closely he would've missed it. What was going on between Rusty and her dad?

"I can be professional. Dad can too," she said. Except her grimace said otherwise.

"If you don't mind my asking—"

"I do."

Damn she was as prickly as a porcupine with a sore paw.

Will let out a pent-up breath. "Holly says you're good…"

He ran a hand around the back of his neck. Was he really considering taking her on, even after their far-from-normal encounters this past week? The situation with Holly didn't leave him much choice. Or was he making up excuses to say yes because part of him wanted to keep Rusty around?

"You won't regret it."

Will glanced up to encounter eyes that glittered with a need to prove something. Prove herself. Even in the shadows, he could see it.

As a rancher with a family going back generations, but who wanted to change things up from how his parents had done it, he got it. Having met her father, who was definitely a son of a bitch, he suspected, for Rusty, that need went deeper.

Finally, he nodded. "Let's spend some time together this week. Talk horses, maybe let me see you work with Mischief, see how our methods match up and if we can work together without you calling me an asshole again."

She winced. "Yeah. Sorry about that."

He raised his eyebrows in question and she sighed.

"I've been burned by a couple of guys who pretended to be interested in me in order to get in with my dad."

Her explanation came out through slightly clenched teeth. Definite sore spot.

Well, that explained a lot. "I wouldn't do that," he promised.

She cocked her head, eyeing him in a wary way that at least now he understood.

He held out a hand. "Let's see how this week goes, then we'll go from there. Deal?"

Again, she nibbled at her lower lip, seeming to consider that promise carefully. After a second, she held out her hand. "Deal."

He curled his around hers to shake, doing his damndest not to register how much softer she felt in his grasp, how tiny and yet strong.

White teeth flashed in a genuine smile, and he sucked in a breath. "You won't regret this," she said.

He let her go. *I just might.*

Chapter Five

RUSTY FOCUSED ON keeping Mischief steady as they waited their turn to run. She'd asked for a slack event on day one, and gotten it. The time between rides would give her long enough to get up to Rising Star, pack her stuff, and get back to Cheyenne for her next round, and, with any luck, the short go.

Nothing could beat the feel of a horse between her legs all revved up and ready to turn and burn that cloverleaf pattern. She kept a tight rein on Mischief as he pranced around to the long chute, eager and trying to go without her. They were up next.

A quick peek in the stands, which were mostly empty as the rodeo show nights wouldn't start for another couple of days. But she couldn't miss the black hat perched on her new boss' head. He sat in the front row, alone, watching every move she was about to make.

"No pressure," she muttered.

Mischief's ears twitched back to her then forward again. Over the loud speakers the announcer's voice blared, and she pulled her gaze off the cowboy.

"Up next, we have Rusty Walker of Rising Star Ranch out of Elk, Wyoming. Rusty was our champion barrel racer three years ago on Butterfinger. Today she's riding Mischief Maker from High Hill Ranch. Let's see what time Rusty gives us today."

Rusty took a deep breath, giving Mischief more of his head as they inched closer to where she'd let him loose. She mentally ran through the run one last time. As one of the earlier contenders, she needed to set the bar. Any time under 17:55 should get her to the second round later in the week.

The announcer finished and she heeled Mischief, throwing her hands forward. The horse, already raring to go, leapt into a hard gallop. He flew across the soft dirt of the arena, barely needing her direction to hit the first barrel. She and her horse fed off each other's energy, perfectly tuned to each other. Powerful hind quarters under him, Mischief pivoted around the obstacle before sprinting toward the next one. A quick lead change and they barely pulled up, Rusty shifted her weight both to help her horse and to keep from being thrown as they circled the second barrel in another fast pivot. With a flick of her heels, she spurred him on toward the third barrel, and around, then rode for the gate, her legs flying, flicking him with reins once, twice. Once they were through the final gate, she pulled Mischief up sharply.

"Seventeen point forty-two ladies and gentlemen. Rusty Walker has come to compete. We'd better keep an eye on this horse and rider combo moving forward."

Yes. Rusty punched a fist in the air.

That time was better than she'd been going for, though Mischief could do it even faster. If she could put up another time in the seventeen-second space on her next round, she'd definitely move on to the short go.

A piercing whistle caught her attention and she turned in the saddle to find Will on his feet, fingers to his lips. When he saw her looking, his teeth flashed white in his suntanned face. The fact she wanted to grin back and wave at him like a loon, had Rusty pulling that reaction back almost as sharply as she'd just reined in Mischief. She nodded at Will instead, then concentrated on getting Mischief out of the way so the next competitor could try to keep up with them.

She rode him to the corral where she walked him in circles, cooling him down from his hard run.

"Damn, girl," a female voice called out. "You trying to set the arena on fire or something?"

A glance in the direction of the sound showed Maggie standing on the bottom rail of the metal corral fence. Rusty laughed as she nudged Mischief to walk over. "I'm making sure we make the finals. Call it a job interview."

Maggie's black brows winged high. "Job? Are you leaving Rising Star? I didn't think you'd ever even consider it."

Rusty shrugged. "I finally realized I need to stand on my own two feet for… a while." Thanks to a brain tumor and a marriage ultimatum. She still hadn't let herself sit down and truly absorb those truths, focusing instead on getting this job.

Maggie tipped her head. "Good for you. So what job are you aiming for?"

"That was a fantastic run, Ms. Walker."

Rusty jumped a bit in the saddle, turning to face Will, who'd managed to sneak up on them. "Thanks. I wanted to make sure I qualified for the next rounds."

He nodded solemnly, his hypnotic blue eyes, so stark in the tan of his face, pulled her in like tractor beams. She shook off the feeling.

"You certainly did that," he said. "Mind if I walk you back to your trailer so we can talk?"

Rusty glanced at Maggie who'd watched the exchange quietly, a small smile tugging at her lips. "I see how the wind's blowing. Talk to you later." She hopped down from the fence and scooted away.

Seeing no way out of talking to Will, Rusty dismounted and led Mischief to the gate, her boots sinking into the thick, soft dirt with each step, kicking dust up to join the dust covering her from their run.

By the time she got there, Will already had it open for her. Hard not to feel petite when standing between a horse and six-foot-three of lean cowboy. Again with the inappropriate reaction to a man about to be her boss. She forced her focus and landed somewhere else… his shirt. Another funny one. This one was navy with yellow text printed sideways that read "You look funny doing that with your head." What was with this guy and funny shirts?

After locking the gate behind her, they walked to the barn where she was keeping Mischief in an assigned stall. She didn't have her big sleeping trailer with her this time. Good thing too, since the ranch owned that trailer, not her. Rusty tugged her hat a little lower over her eyes.

At the stall, she and Will worked in a surprisingly comfortable silence. He pulled off her saddle while she haltered the horse and tied him up to brush him down. Will also grabbed a brush, working from the other side.

"I know Holly trained him to primarily respond to leg commands, but I saw you using the reins a bit more."

Rusty nodded. "Her technique for teaching him to bend around the barrels, using the inside leg almost like an anchor is fantastic, but he needed a little more direction between barrels and to get his speed up."

"So if you're training for us, what's your method?"

Let the interview begin. Still, even through her tension, Rusty could breathe. This was her favorite thing to talk about on the planet. She could go on for days.

"Each horse is different," she started. "The trick is figuring out what works best for that horse then finding him a rider that matches personality and style."

"So, you don't mind learning new techniques?"

"Heck, no. The point is the end result, an animal who can win. And I'll be straight up with you if I think a horse isn't meant to run barrels, or not with the client looking at him."

Will made his way around Mischief's hindquarters. "Do you think some horses are untrainable."

Even Mischief looked around, eyeing her like he had a thing or two to say about that.

Rusty chuckled, patting the handsome horse's soft red neck under his black mane. "Of course not. If they're not a good barrel runner, that doesn't mean they can't be good for something else. I know you do a lot of stock horse breeding and training."

"That's good to hear," Will murmured, but suddenly closer than she'd expected.

She turned away from Mischief to find Will had worked his way to her while she was talking. A bit too close. She could practically feel the warmth from his body, even in the already sweltering July heat wave taking over Cheyenne.

But she refused to show she was riled, refused to step back. *Bet he's just trying to mess me up on purpose.*

She shrugged and concentrated on finishing with Mischief. "I do my research."

"So, what would you most want to be involved in at High Hill?"

Rusty paused. No one had ever asked that before.

She finished one last stroke then dumped the brush into the bucket. "Barrel racing is obviously a passion. I'm also great with steer ropers and stock horses, of course. I'd also be happy to work with Western show horses, not so much dressage. I can do jumpers, but my experience there is limited."

She led Mischief into his stall and Will closed the door behind her as she stepped out. Again, too close for her peace of mind.

"And how many can you take on at once?" he asked next.

"I like to warm up and cool down the horses." Before he could argue, she held up a hand. "I know that means less horses a day, but that time with them lets me gain their trust, which I think is important."

"I wasn't going to say anything." She caught the hint of amusement, but at least he didn't smirk or laugh. Condescending males were one of her hot buttons.

Rusty sidestepped him, irritated with needing a little breathing space. "Sorry. Dad thinks that's wasted time, since we have grooms and folks who can do it for me."

Will walked with her toward the door. "Everyone has their own method. I asked what works for you."

"Right. Well, if I'm doing that, then I can handle as many as six, maybe eight a day. I give every horse a day or two off a week. Which means if I'm riding six a day, I can work with about seven horses total, assuming I'm taking one day off a week myself."

"Sounds about right," was all he said.

She paused and glanced at him, waiting for a comment or sign of sarcasm. Was this guy for real? She was not used to such a laid-back style. Her father, or even the boys who worked for him, would've butted in a hundred times by now with their own thoughts on the matter.

She blinked in the sun as they emerged from the shadows of the barn. "Any concerns?"

He raised his eyebrows. "Not so far."

He must've caught her skeptical look because he chuckled. "I'll try to think of a few over lunch."

Lunch?

Oblivious to her surprise that they were having lunch, he continued. "None of my stock is competing today, and I assume you're done. How about we head over to Hanovers and continue this discussion. My treat?"

"Fine by me." *Not a date, not date, not a date.* She mentally repeated the mantra to herself. She made a show of checking her watch. "I have to leave by one, though."

"Got somewhere to be?"

"Quick trip to Rising Star. I need to pack up."

She didn't miss the way his brows drew down in a tiny frown. Was that concern? She might be jumping the gun with this job, but if it didn't work out that didn't matter. She'd find another. No way was she staying with her father after his most recent ultimatum.

She waited for the probing questions from Will.

"Are you taking Mischief with you?" was all he asked.

Relief trickled through her along with surprise. "No. My friend Maggie's going to look after him. I'll be back by tomorrow."

"Sounds like a plan."

Seriously? That was it? No demanding she take someone with her? Or insisting she needed to stay here to watch her horse, which was really his sister-in-law's horse? No reminder that he hadn't hired her yet, either. Huh.

She went to turn left toward the lot where she'd parked, but he hooked her by the elbow, tugging her the other way. "I'm in B Lot," he said.

"I can meet you there."

"Nah. We can talk on the way, then I'll drop you at your truck when we're done."

Alone in the cab of his truck. Why the heck did that have her all fluttery? She'd been alone with lots of men in trucks and never thought twice about it. Part of her wanted to dig in her heels and insist on meeting him there, but that would be silly.

"Rusty!"

No mistaking that voice. She and Will both paused and turned around to see Dave making his way to them at a brisk walk.

He eyed Will as he caught up with them, but addressed her. "Your dad is looking for you."

She tried not to let her irritation show in front of Will. "I have a cell phone, Dave. If Dad needs to talk to me, he can call and arrange a time."

Dave's mouth dropped open for a second. No surprise. Despite the little rebellions like the pink, girly clothes and calling him Daddy, Rusty usually ran to do her father's bidding, wanting to earn his approval. Not anymore.

"But he's waiting," Dave said.

"And I have a meeting right now. He should've checked with me."

She went to turn away, only to have Dave grab her wrist. "I can't let you leave, Rusty."

Will said nothing, but he stepped closer to her and Dave flicked him a wary glance. Still he didn't let go. "I'm supposed to look out for you."

She twisted out of his grip. "Didn't you hear? I'm leaving Rising Star. You'll just have to do your job instead, and that no longer involves looking out for me."

Poor Dave stood there like a deer on the highway about to be smacked by an eighteen-wheeler. Which was probably close to the truth. She didn't envy him having to deliver this message to Garrett Walker. Dave had only been doing what the boss said, after all. Even if he'd been a twerp about it.

She patted his arm. "You could tell Dad you never found me."

He let out a huffing laugh. "Yes, ma'am. That might be best." He tipped his hat to her and Will and walked off the way he'd come.

"What was that about?" Will asked.

She sighed, really not wanting to get into the entire drama with her potential new boss. "I think Dad is experiencing some separation anxiety."

Deliberately, she played it down. Her daddy issues weren't anyone's business but hers anyway.

WILL HELD THE truck door open for Rusty and did his best to keep his eyes off her backside, so nicely displayed in her riding jeans. Today she wore a black western style shirt with a hot pink design across the shoulders and back and at the cuff of her sleeves, with sparkles of course.

"You sure like pink," he said.

She plunked that fine backside in her seat and looked at him.

Embarrassed at letting his mouth speak before his brain engaged, Will indicated her shirt with a wave. "I haven't seen you in another color is all, if you don't count the black."

When she didn't look like she was going to answer, he closed the door and walked around to his side of the truck.

He'd cranked the engine when she spoke. "My father only wanted boys."

He paused with his hand on the gear shift to glance her way.

Her lips pursed, like she was trying to hold back the words. Will waited. Rusty Walker reminded him of a filly he'd once worked with. She'd been abused by her previous owner and was skittish around everyone and everything. Quiet patience had eventually won her over.

"You could say that he's a man's man and only thinks men have anything of value to offer."

Will could read between the lines—a chauvinist father couldn't be easy for a girl, but especially one with strength and a backbone, like Rusty. "So the pink is you thumbing your nose at him?" he asked.

She flicked him a wide-eyed glance, her deep brown eyes reflecting her surprise, and laughed. "Good guess. More like reminding him that I'm not a son. After my brother Reed died, Dad tried his hardest to make me into one."

That was right. The Walkers had had a son. He vaguely thought he and her brother had been about the same age, but growing up in Wyoming and Texas, their paths hadn't crossed. Will'd only been doing local rodeos then, but as he'd grown his business, he'd heard something about that. "I'm sorry. About your brother…"

She shifted uncomfortably in her seat. "Thanks. He was sort of great."

Time to lighten things up. He put the truck in gear. "I'm also sorry you had to wear pink all the time."

Her chuckle went straight to his crotch and it tightened uncomfortably. He could deal with that, but what had Will a bit worried was the fact he liked making Rusty loosen up enough to laugh with him. That could get addictive real quick. Too quick.

At Hanovers, she sat across from him. They ordered from the waitress who popped by. Will changed his mind about his order when Rusty got the chicken fried chicken, because getting the same thing was way too cutesy. So he went with his second choice of steak.

"Tell me about your operation," Rusty said as she settled back against her chair.

A topic that was safe ground. Will leaned forward, elbows propped on the table. "High Hill Ranch has been in my family for generations. It's located in the Texas Hill Country, south of Fredericksburg and west of Austin. The closest town is La Colina. We run cattle primarily, but also some sheep and goats because they take advantage of some of the rougher, higher terrain in the hills that the cattle won't climb up to."

"Smart," she murmured.

Will shrugged. "You gotta work with what you're dealt."

She nodded, and he continued. "I'm one of five siblings, but only three of us have stuck around to run the ranch. My younger brothers, Autry and Jennings, both work with Dad handling the cattle side of things."

"Except the rodeo stock?" she asked.

"Right. Those fall under my side of the business. I'm most focused on the horses—training in various events as well as working stock. But to get into rodeo, as you know, it helps to have the bulls too."

Rusty leaned in, and Will tracked the change in her demeanor. Talk about horses and she forgot to be so wary, opening up in a way that lightened her expression. For a moment, she was that woman in the truck dancing like no one was watching. What would it take to get her to be like that with him all the time?

"Is there a particular sport or event you're focusing on?" she asked, unaware of his mental musings.

Damn, she was gorgeous. And so obviously didn't realize the effect she could have on a man. Maybe that was a good thing, or she could wrap him around her little finger with ease. Will shifted, uncomfortable with that thought, and pushed it aside.

He shook his head. "I go where the money is, if it makes business sense. Stock horses and rodeo stock are my current big-ticket items. I'm hoping to expand those, as well as branch into other areas."

And barrel racers made sense. It was a niche market, but depending on the stock and their reputation, they could sell green horses for around five thousand dollars, higher level riders would often pay as much as thirty thousand dollars for an almost finished trained horse, and the pros had been known to pay as much as a hundred grand for a fully trained horse. Not to mention lessons, and other opportunities. But Will didn't ride or train barrel racers, which was why he'd pulled Holly into his operation. And now Rusty.

He let his gaze trail over her features. Stubborn chin, slightly tip-tilted nose, kissable pink lips, and freckles dusted across her skin going with the deep red hair she currently had pulled back in a French braid. She was a petite thing, but by the way she rode, she was also all muscle.

And damned if that wasn't attractive as sin.

Crap. Keep your mind on the conversation, buddy.

The waitress picked an opportune moment, showing up with their food. Will welcomed the distraction as he tucked into his steak, then glanced up to find Rusty devouring hers.

He grinned. "Hungry?"

She smiled around a bite. "I'm always hungry after a ride. The adrenaline, I guess."

And, if she was anything like Holly, she probably couldn't eat before, although he'd bet Rusty would never admit to nerves like that.

"What do your other siblings do?" she asked.

Will blinked at her, lost in the change of conversation.

She waved her fork. "You said you had four siblings, but only two of your brothers are at the ranch. What about the other two?"

Ah. "Cash is married to Holly. He's the sheriff in La Colina County. She's one of the large animal vets in the area. They live in town."

She kept eating, but was obviously listening.

"Carter is the only girl. She and Cash are twins. She got all the brains and is in the middle of her PhD work in hydrologic science and water management."

Rusty's eyebrows winged high. "Wow. Sounds complicated."

"You'll have to ask her what it's all about. Something to

do with water distribution across the country and rights management. She says water is the next crisis."

Way to bring it back down to a low note. He gave a mental shake of his head.

"Wait." Rusty cocked her head. "Cash, Carter, Jennings…" A twinkle entered her deep brown eyes. "You're not all named after—"

"Classic country music stars?" Will grimaced. "Yeah."

Her smile widened. "That's fun. Let me guess."

He waved at her to go ahead, and she took a second to think about it. "Johnny Cash and June Carter for the twins obviously. And Waylon Jennings?"

She glanced at him for confirmation, and he nodded. "Jennings is the youngest."

"Autry… Gene Autry?"

Will smiled. "Yup. Second youngest, and the wildest of the bunch. Watch out when you come work for us. He'd charm the skin off a rattlesnake."

Rusty rolled her eyes. "I'm not in the market for a boyfriend anyway." She eyed him speculatively.

"What?"

"I'm trying to figure out your name. All the others use last names. But Will…" She shook her head, thinking hard. "Willie Nelson maybe?"

"Nope. Do you want a hint?"

She held up a hand. "I'll get there on my own."

He suspected that was Rusty Walker's personal mantra.

She gasped. "Hank Williams? Your name is Williams?"

Will tipped his water at her. "Yes, ma'am."

"And do they all look like you?" The second the question was out, Rusty scrunched up her nose, the expression adorably irritated.

Had she not meant to ask that? Interesting.

"Like me?" He couldn't resist prodding.

She cleared her throat. "You know. Tall. Dark hair." Her gaze trailed over him, and Will swore he felt that look like a caress. Now he was imagining things.

"Blue eyes." She tacked on, husky voice dropping a note.

Then she seemed to give herself a shake. Maybe he wasn't imagining things? He pretended not to notice, despite the way his body hardened at the thought of her reciprocal interest.

"We all got my dad's coloring, the Hill coloring, which apparently goes back generations—dark hair and blue eyes. Except Autry, he got Mom's hazel eyes."

"I can't imagine growing up with so many siblings," she murmured. "I had Reed around, but he died when I was only eleven. After that, it was just me. Dad laid off anyone who married and had a kid, insisting family men were distracted workers. So there weren't any kids to play with on the ranch, only at school."

That had to be a lonely existence. "I can't imagine life without them. Don't get me wrong, we quarreled, and I've had my fair share of black eyes from a tussle or two." Given them out too, not that he was proud of that fact. "But I know my family have my back. We support each other."

Rusty was quiet a long moment, toying with her iced tea, making the sweat gathering on the outside of the plastic cup bead up and drip to the coaster. "We all walk a different path, I guess. Mine made me who I am. Yours did, too."

Will stayed silent, sensing Rusty wasn't too happy. With the comment or the path her life had her on up to this point, he wasn't sure which. Maybe both.

Finally, she lifted her chocolate eyes.

Finding his gaze on her, she sat up taller. "You done with your steak?" She nodded at his plate.

Will cleared his throat and also sat forward. "Yes, ma'am."

Rusty scrunched up her nose again. What did he do this time? When she caught his questioning look, eyebrows raised, she did it again. "Please don't call me ma'am," she said.

"My mama raised me right," he replied. "And it's just old-fashioned manners."

She huffed a laugh. "I'm not objecting to the manners. But ma'am makes me feel about a hundred years old."

The woman in front of him—vital and colorful and… beautiful—was so far from an old maid Will had to laugh. "Okay. No more ma'ams," he agreed.

Only she didn't laugh with him. She blinked like she'd realized something, or had been surprised by something maybe. Either way, her stare ratcheted his own tension up another couple of notches. What would she do if he leaned across the table and kissed her right now? No excuse about helping her with a drunk, just a guy wanting to kiss a girl.

The waitress chose that moment to pop by. "Either of you up for dessert?"

Rusty's eyes lit up. "What's good?"

"Depends on if you're a chocolate dessert lover or fruit."

"Definitely chocolate."

"Then the s'mores pie is the way I'd go."

Rusty smiled. "You had me at chocolate."

Will shook his head when the waitress turned to him. She left and the same tension she'd interrupted returned. He needed to do something to break it. "My family are the reason I need to succeed."

She dropped her gaze to the table where she fiddled with her glass. "Because you're not continuing with the traditional ranching?"

She glanced up and Will nodded. "My family believes in me. They've sunk a lot of money into my new business, and my father and two brothers are doing all the other work while I get things running. I can't let them down. Do you understand?"

Her lips twisted in a strangely bitter smile. "More than you know."

Why? Because of her father? He had a feeling she knew a lot about trying to prove herself. He just hoped she'd direct that fire toward helping him. Like she said.

The waitress interrupted again to place Rusty's pie in front of her. Rusty took one bite and groaned.

Will chuckled. "Good?"

She gave him a sheepish smile over another bite before shoveling it into her mouth. Rusty Walker apparently had a sweet tooth.

She finished chewing and cleared her throat. "If you took me on, I'd do everything in my power to help you with your goals."

Will considered her for a long moment. "I believe you."

She stilled. "Good." Rusty waived down the waitress and asked for the check. Then turned to him. "It'll only take me a day to get my things. I'll be back tomorrow about this time."

"When's your next round?"

"Thursday."

Plenty of time. Will paid, then held Rusty's chair out for her. Automatically he reached for her hand to lead her outside, not even thinking about it. His family were huggers and casual touch, to them, was just an everyday thing.

But Rusty twisted out of his grasp and took a few hurried steps to get ahead of him. Apparently, she wasn't a casual touch person, no matter how innocent taking her hand had been. Or maybe not so innocent, because he'd been wanting to touch her since their kiss. Will made a mental note to keep his hands to himself around her. Given his unusual reaction to the woman, that was probably a good idea for him too.

They rode back to the rodeo grounds in silence. She opened the door and hopped out before he'd even shut off the engine. She looked up at him, and suddenly Will didn't want her to leave, even for the day. Which was ridiculous. He tightened his grip on the wheel.

Hell, this is not what I need right now. She was about to be his employee.

"See you tomorrow?" she asked.

He tipped an imaginary hat, his own hat propped on the dash. "I'll be around."

Chapter Six

THE HIGHWAY STRETCHED out before Rusty like a long ribbon of black in the inky night. Rusty blinked away her tiredness and kept her foot on the gas. Not much longer now. She could see the glow of the city on the horizon. She'd get to her room and sleep. Tomorrow she'd worry about things like food and giving Mischief a good workout.

Her phone rang, lighting up the cup holder where she'd stashed it and interrupting the song on the radio. Rusty glanced at the display, but didn't recognize the number, except that it was a Texas number. She flicked her thumb to hit the button on her steering wheel that allowed her to use the truck's Bluetooth to talk.

"Rusty Walker."

"It's Will."

Despite her strict instructions to her body not to respond to Will in any way, shape, or form, her dang heart hadn't paid attention to the lecture, because it sped up at the sound of his deep voice. "Hi, Will."

"I'm just checking in on you. I didn't see you around today."

Was he seriously that nice? Or was he going to turn into another form of babysitter? "I'm still on the road," she said.

"Did you get everything packed up okay?"

"Yeah. It took a little longer than I expected." Turned out when she lived her entire life in mostly one place, college being her only time away from home, she accumulated a ton of stuff.

That and she'd been particular about what she packed, trying to make sure she only took away stuff she'd paid for herself or items that had been gifts. Good thing she had a cover on the bed of the truck, because she'd stuffed it to almost overflowing.

"Where are you now?" he asked next.

Rusty sighed. "I know you're trying to be nice, Will. But I can look after myself."

A pause greeted that statement. "I know that, Rusty."

She pursed her lips at the distance that infused his voice now.

"I was going to pick up some dinner and take it back to the B and B. If you're close enough, I thought you might like some too. Save you the trip."

Rusty's stomach rumbled at the very thought of food. She was tired enough, and it was late enough, she'd written off the idea of dinner. But after she'd just played the independent bitch card, it seemed hypocritical to take him up on the offer. "I'll grab something later."

"Sounds good." Another pause. "Your friend Maggie did

well tonight."

"Yeah?" she asked. Was it sad she was glad he hadn't hung up? The long drive—away from her home and her hopes—must be making her feel lonely.

"She didn't quite hit your time, but she's close. You two are top of the leader board at the moment."

Rusty straightened at that. "That's terrific. Now if I can turn in a good run on Thursday, Holly will be in some good money."

"Yup. Well, I guess I'll see you tomorrow."

She refused to acknowledge the twinge of disappointment that he was hanging up. She was just lonely on the solitary drive. "Sounds good. Night, Will."

"Night."

She pushed the button to end the call, and the music came back over the speakers. An hour later, she gratefully parked her truck in the street outside the Victorian house where she and Will were staying. She left all her stuff in the back, locked under the cover and grabbed her purse. She'd left her gear while she'd been gone, so she didn't even need to bring in a suitcase.

Bleary from the drive, her steps dragging, she hauled her butt into the house and up the three flights of stairs where she let herself into her room. She'd chosen this place on a whim. The idea at the time had been to get away from motels and her father's watch dogs.

She was glad she had. The small room was all understated grace with tan and white wallpaper, and a tasteful white bedspread on the antique iron bed. French-style doors opened up to a private bath that included a six-foot-long, claw-foot tub.

Now she eyed the tub, debating if she was so tired she might accidentally fall asleep in the water if she drew a bath. But her muscles were so stiff from sitting in one position for hours, the idea appealed. She gave in, and fifteen minutes later sighed with pleasure as the hot water soothed away two days of travel and packing and a hard goodbye to her old life.

She was about to drag herself out of the water, which was turning lukewarm anyway, when a knock sounded at her door. With a groan, she hauled herself up, and wrapped a towel around her body. "Yes?" she called to whoever was on the other side of the door.

"It's Will."

Her eyes went wide. "Oh! Um…" She glanced down at her towel. No way was she opening the door to him like this. Way too cliché. "I was in the bath. Give me a second."

Pause. "Sure."

Wide awake now, and frustrated as hell that her heart was doing that fluttery thing again, Rusty rushed through dressing, throwing on her PJs, which constituted a black T-shirt with words in pink that read "Please don't make me adult today." And matching pink shorts. The outfit was modest enough, but she added a bra, because answering him without one seemed like asking for trouble. Her hair she left piled on top of her head where she'd twisted it up in topknot for her bath.

A quick glance around her room, which was in good order, and she swung the door open to find Will standing there holding bags of food.

Her breath whooshed from her as his gaze traveled slowly down her body. Maybe the PJs had been a bad idea. The way his eyes lingered on her legs, and the deep V of the shirt had her shivering in stark reaction. His mouth quirked as he read the words printed across her chest.

Then he blinked, and all the heat she thought she'd seen in his deep blue gaze seemed to disappear. Maybe wishful thinking had put it there in the first place.

He held up the bags. "I got a little extra food just in case. You hungry?"

"Not really." Unfortunately, probably thanks to the mouthwatering scent of BBQ, her stomach chose that moment to grumble rather loudly about the lack of food in it.

Rather than let Will comment, she sighed, and stepped back. "Come on in."

To his credit, he contained a grin she was sure hid behind lips pressed tightly together, and didn't comment as he stepped inside. He immediately moved to the small writing desk, the only table in the room, and started unloading cartons of food.

"I didn't realize how much they were going to give me,"

he said. "No way could I have finished this on my own."

She raised her eyes at the containers of brisket, smoked turkey, and sausage, along with several sides like potato salad and coleslaw. "Did you buy the entire store?" she teased.

He shrugged. "I think my eyes were bigger than my stomach."

She pulled out the delicate wooden chair and sat down, leaving him to take the larger armchair which was more likely to support his greater bulk. They were quiet for a few minutes while they loaded their paper plates with food and dug in.

Two meals in two days. If she wasn't careful, she'd start thinking of these as dates.

Rusty opened her mouth to make some kind of random comment to break the silence, but he beat her to it.

"So, you like funny T-shirts?" he asked.

She slow blinked, trying to track with the topic, and he waved at her PJ top.

"Oh," she said. "I have a few, I guess. Not as many as you apparently."

He flicked her a half-sheepish, half-amused smile "You noticed those, huh?"

"Kinda hard to miss." She waved at today's example which read "Sprinkles are for winners."

"Yeah." He took a bite of BBQ and carefully chewed. Was that a... was he blushing?

"What's the story with those?" she pushed.

He gave a small huff of a sigh. "My family gets them for me as gifts."

"And…" She had no idea how she knew there was more, but she did.

He raised his eyebrows, but still answered. "They tease me that I have no sense of humor and so they use the T-shirts to teach me how to be funny."

"Huh. Seems to me your sense of humor is just fine."

"Thanks," he muttered. "Did you get everything packed up okay?"

Rusty stiffened, but a glance at his face showed only general curiosity. She wanted to shake her head. She'd never encountered anyone as seemingly laid-back and up front as Williams Hill. She found him surprisingly easy to be around, despite the annoying way her body perked up in his presence.

"It was harder than I expected it to be." She found herself confessing.

He was mid-chew of food, but raised his eyebrows in question.

"A lot of memories to be walking away from." She tried for a nonchalant shrug. Why had she laid that on him? It wasn't his problem.

"I bet," he said. At least he didn't seem too concerned about the heavy topic. "I couldn't imagine moving. Other than college, I've lived in the same room in my parents' house since I was born, practically."

"Me, too."

"If you accumulate half the stuff I do, you had a lot to pack up."

Except she doubted he'd be worried about sifting out the items that his parents would hold over his head as not really his. Living out from under her father's thumb, if not the shadow of his legacy and now his impending passing, would be weird. That was for sure.

"Your father cornered me today." He suddenly dropped into the conversation.

"Oh?" She tried not to make a face. After all, she'd promised Will's business with her dad wouldn't be a problem.

"Yeah." He rubbed a hand over his jaw, the scratch of the stubble loud in the otherwise quiet room. "He demanded to know if I'd hired you."

Rusty curled her hands into fists. Was her dad going to block her attempts to be independent now? "And what'd you say?"

"I told him I had."

That didn't necessarily mean anything. "Was he mad?"

Will's lips thinned, those blue eyes of his darkening as he frowned. "You could say that."

He stood and started gathering the remains of their food. Rusty couldn't eat any more anyway. Not with her mind on Will's encounter with her father. That was it? Where was the yelling? Or telling her this wasn't going to work out?

She got to her feet to help him. "You don't seem too concerned."

"I'm not. Yet."

Rusty wrestled with the lid to the potato salad, her inner turmoil coming out in an inability to win the skirmish with the plastic. Will stacked all the containers into the plastic bag, then stopped and covered her hands, ending her agitated movements. She stilled under his touch, warm and solid.

"Rusty," he murmured.

She lifted her gaze to his to find kindness in his eyes, something she hadn't encountered in a long time.

"Would it be easier if I knew the situation? In order to deal with him?"

She'd already been considering telling him. After all, given his position, smack between her and her father, it was only fair.

She took a deep breath. "My father is dying."

Will blinked a couple of times and she gave him a moment to process. "I'm sorry to hear that," he finally said.

She bit her lip, trying to hold back frustratingly useless tears that stung the back of her eyes. "Thanks. He just told me the other day. An inoperable brain tumor."

"I see." Will ran a hand through his hair, ruffling it up. "Forgive me for saying this, but shouldn't you be staying with him?"

Normally, she'd take that as judgmental, but only kind curiosity looked back at her. "I should. And I would. Except…"

Oh, Lord. Was she going to have to admit to this humiliating situation?

"Except?" Will asked.

"He's demanding I get married. He's going to change his will so that I only inherit if I've married a man he approves of."

"What?" The question punched from Will so loudly that she jumped.

She waved a hand, shushing him.

"Are you kidding me?" he asked in more hushed tones.

She gave a humorless laugh. "I wish I were. But, nope. When I refused, he kicked me off the property… and here we are." She waved a hand between them.

To her shock, Will started pacing back and forth in front of her. "I've never heard of anything so… ridiculous." He flung out an arm in his agitation.

Barbaric. Arcane. Dictatorial. Controlling. Rusty'd thrown every one of those words at the situation already. "Tell me about it."

"He'll let the ranch go to some stranger instead of his own daughter?"

"Not a stranger. Apparently, he's picked out a suitable person who knows the industry." She air quoted those last words.

"But you know the industry. That much is obvious, and I've only known you a little while."

And kissed her. Was about to become her boss.

Rusty shrugged. "I appreciate your concern, Will. But I know my father. There's no changing his mind."

He paced for another second before stopping directly in front of her, close enough she could smell the spicy scent of his aftershave. With effort, she held her ground.

Will put his hands on her shoulders. "You have a job with High Hill. And don't worry about my business with your dad. Okay?"

Only he didn't know Garrett Walker like she did. Still, something about the steady strength staring down at her settled the churning in her gut. "Okay," she whispered.

Silence and a heady awareness settled between them and she continued to gaze up at Will. They didn't move. She should look away, say something to break the moment, but she couldn't. Didn't want to.

Before she could talk herself out of it, before the moment ended, Rusty went up on tiptoe. She put her hand against his cheek and placed her lips over his in a sweet kiss, one that lingered as reluctance to pull away held her there.

When she pulled away, his hands remained on her hips as he searched her eyes. "What was that for?" he asked.

"You're a good man, Williams Hill. Don't ever let anyone tell you otherwise."

His jaw worked under her hand, the one still resting against the warm skin of his cheek, his stubble rasping against her skin. "Don't fit me for a halo yet," he said.

"No?" she smiled. "Why not?"

"Because of this…"

With strong hands at her hips, he drew her against the lean length of his body, lowering his lips to hers. Only his kiss wasn't sweet, wasn't anywhere close to sweet. He claimed, his tongue flicking the seam of her lips, demanding entrance, which she willingly gave.

Nice men weren't supposed to kiss like this, she vaguely thought as she surrendered her body to his power. Every part of her was tuned to him, to the brush of his hands against her waist, to every slide of his lips and tongue as they tangled with hers, feeding the heat blooming low inside her.

Slowly, the tenor of his kisses changed, softening as Will slowed them down, then pulled back. Rusty kept her eyes closed, taking a second to catch her breath before she opened them to find him regarding her with a small frown marring his brow.

"I shouldn't have done that," he said.

Disappointment sank through her to settle in her toes, which she curled into the thick rug under her feet. "Why not?"

He stepped back and ran an agitated hand through his hair. Hair she'd just had her hands speared through she realized, as memories of the silky texture registered.

"I'm your boss, now," he said. "That makes things… different."

Talk about dousing heat with a bucket of iced water. At

least that was how it felt to Rusty. She also took a step back. "That's right. You're right. We shouldn't…"

And now she was a mumbling mess. Terrific.

"It won't happen again," he said.

"Fine." To end the awkward moment, she gathered up the plastic bags of food and handed them over to him. "Thanks for dinner."

He paused, mouth open like he wanted to say more, but must've read her closed expression correctly, because he let out a short breath. "Good night, Rusty. See you tomorrow."

She might've muttered a good night in return. Rusty honestly didn't know. She just wanted him out of her room so she could die of embarrassment in private. She walked him to the door, locking it behind him.

Then she leaned against the door and touched her lips which still tingled from his kisses.

Hellfire and damnation. What had she been thinking?

She shook her head. She wasn't thinking, because Will could kiss a nun out of her habit. That was what happened. Definitely not the best start to a boss-employee relationship. He'd been right about that.

She drew her shoulders back and pushed off the door. With mechanical motions, she went about getting ready for bed. From now on, it was professional only with Will. She was a strong, independent woman, so she could handle that.

As she turned off the light, the little devil who periodically popped up on her shoulder dropped by to laugh in her face, because her body still hummed with unrealized need for the man sleeping across the hall from her. She ignored the devil and shut her eyes.

WILL SPENT THE next days calling himself all sorts of fool and keeping his hands well away from Rusty. He hadn't offered to bring her food again, either. Clearly, being alone in her bedroom had been a horrible plan. So he kept it professional.

He'd observed her working Mischief on Wednesday. On Thursday, she cemented her position at the top of the leader board with another fantastic run on Holly's horse, which also put her in the short go. She sat with him in the stands to watch the steer ropers he'd trained in action, discussing the finer points of training horses for that type of work. She'd even hung out with him behind the scenes as he helped prep his bulls for their rides.

Will had wanted to tell every single cowboy who glanced her way to keep his dang eyes to himself. And there were a lot of them. Her red hair acted like a beacon, and the rest of the package was about as enticing as it got. However, he hadn't needed to go all caveman and give them the stink eye, because Rusty took care of it for him. She didn't seem to notice most of the stares, but when she did catch a more blatant one she'd stare right back with an expression that clearly said, "Move along. You have zero chance here."

After a while, the guys had left her to her own devices, which seemed to suit Rusty just fine. Him too. Meanwhile, going on about his business had been harder than normal, thanks to the thoughts in his head.

Those were anything but professional. Because a crazy idea had taken root. One which he debated on an off nonstop as the rodeo went on. Even Chris and Jordan had noticed his distraction.

"What's with you, boss?" Jordan had asked this morning.

"What do you mean?" Will asked.

"I mean a prime opportunity to sell the cowboy a horse just walked away, and you didn't even notice."

Will grimaced again. He hadn't been paying any attention to the conversation with that cowboy. Hell, now that redhead was messing with his business. But he couldn't seem to let go of that crazy idea.

The logical, no-nonsense part of him wanted to believe it was all about business. Rusty would be much easier to partner with than her father. If he could help Rusty in a very specific way—one that guaranteed her Rising Star—then, quid pro quo, she could partner with him. He'd give her better access to the Texas circuit. In the Midwest and mountain areas, not only would Rising Star get him access, but they could handle the transport and care of the animals more efficiently and on a larger scale than he was currently set up to do. More business. Win-win.

However, a part down deep he really didn't want to listen to shouted at him, like hearing a tiny voice calling from the bottom of a well, that he might've fallen for Rusty Walker the minute he saw her ride, and that was what was driving this need to help her. Which was head over heels ridiculous.

Harebrained, his mother would call it. Still... the more he debated, silencing that inner voice, the more he thought it could work.

Right now, he stood on a rung of the corral fence, arms looped over the top as he watched her work with Maggie and her horse. In the distance, he could hear the roar of the crowd, the boom of the announcer's voice, and the periodic music over the loudspeakers.

That was one thing about the rodeo life. The fans in the stands only saw the excitement of what was going on in the arena, but for the folks behind the scenes, most of the time was spent waiting. Lots and lots of waiting.

The last day of the rodeo and he had three bulls riding, as well as two of his roping horses still in it, and Rusty was riding Mischief, of course.

Barrel racing was up in half an hour or so, and Mischief stood quietly beside Will, hitched to the fence while Rusty and Maggie worked. Maggie claimed her horse was pulling to the left, and had asked Rusty's advice. Which presented the perfect opportunity for him to observe how she'd work with potential clients and other horses.

Crud. No way could he pull off the strictly professional thing with her. He was hard just standing here watching her work the horse. Yet another check in the crazy idea column.

Granted, thanks to more than one cold shower, he'd kept a repeat of the other night from happening. In fact, if anything, an easy camaraderie had fallen between them. One of Will's favorite people was his brother Cash's new wife, Holly, because she was as horse crazy as he was. They could talk horse for hours. He found the same to be true of Rusty, who not only loved horses, but had spent her entire life around them and around rodeo. Hell, she'd probably learned to ride before she could walk.

Granted, he'd never once had the urge to kiss Holly, and in quiet moments sitting together or moments like last night when the Turtle had earned his highest score yet and he'd swept Rusty up in an exuberant hug, the thing between them made itself felt. Even now, he couldn't keep his gaze from moving over her backside as she mounted. Hell, the woman had curves for such a petite thing. A fact he knew from firsthand experience, having run his hands over the indent of her waist and down those soft hips.

Get your mind off her ass. You're her boss. Keep it professional.

With effort, he pulled his concentration back to what she was doing and saying. He kept quiet and observed for the half-hour or so it took the women to discuss everything, watching as Rusty cantered Maggie's horse, Galant, then did a few slow curves around barrels.

After they wrapped up, he tipped his hat in Maggie's direction, then found himself alone with Rusty and Mischief. She untied him from the fence and they walked slowly toward the stadium together, in no particular hurry. The horse's hooves made a hushed clopping in the thick dirt, the sound turning sharper as they exited the barn onto the harder packed dirt between buildings.

"I like the way you work with people," he said.

She laughed. "You thought I'd be bad with them?"

Will grinned. "No. But I'd say you're a woman who doesn't pull her punches. You seem to be a fan of straight talk, but, with Maggie at least, you temper it with patience and understanding that she might have a different approach. It works for you."

She paused and he stopped walking to face her.

"I think that's the first compliment you've given me," she said. "Thanks."

He crossed his arms. "If you wanted compliments, at least ones that don't have to do with your physical assets"—with monumental effort, he kept his gaze from dropping below her eyes—"then you should've picked a different business. Cowboys aren't into spewing pretty words."

Rusty laughed and rolled her eyes. "Duh. Still, that's nice to hear."

They picked back up walking. The air hung still and heavy, no breeze, and Will had to lift his hat to wipe at his forehead with the sleeve of his shirt. At least this was a dry heat. In Texas, he was used to the added discomfort that came with high humidity. He'd be sweating a lot worse in those conditions. Still, that didn't make the sun any less intense.

"I have an idea—" The words popped out of his mouth.

Dammit. He hadn't even been thinking about his crazy plan right then. Had he? Or maybe it was all he'd been thinking about since the night in her room.

She stopped walking to face him. "Yeah?"

Can't back out now. He gazed down at her upturned face—wide brown eyes gazing at him with vague curiosity, a stubborn chin, kissable lips, freckles. A face he wouldn't mind waking up to every morning.

"Marry me," he said.

Holy shit. Now he'd gone and done it. The damned crazy idea was out now.

Rusty's eyes flew wide. "Excuse me?" she asked in a voice that trembled slightly.

He could take it back, say never mind, walk away. Only he found he didn't want to. He wanted her to say yes, the little voice inside him growing louder. This was going to take some fast talking. "Hear me out, okay?"

She seemed too shocked to respond either way, her mouth hanging open in an adorable way he bet didn't happen often with her. He took advantage, breaking into speech.

"You want Rising Star, and the only way to get it is to marry. Why not marry me? I think the last few days have proved we could work well together, and it solves the inheritance problem."

Rusty opened and closed her mouth a few times. Probably not a good sign. Then she scowled. Definitely not a good sign. "When did my father tell you he'd already approved of you as a candidate?"

He had? That was... interesting. "I haven't talked to your father."

"Yeah, right." She turned and tromped away, leading Mischief.

Will caught up to her. "I mean it, Rusty. I haven't talked to him."

She stopped and swung to him so sharply that Will had to hop back a bit. "No?" she demanded. "Then what's in it for you?"

She'd just laugh hysterically in his face and walk away if he said that *she* was what was in it for him. Hell, he was on the verge of thinking he'd lost his mind anyway. *He* hardly believed himself.

So instead he tried to appeal to her logical side, because he still had solid arguments on that side. "There's no denying being linked to Rising Star would be good for my business, too. Access, transportation, care, and so forth. But how about this... we'll draw up a document that says I get no part of the ranch when you inherit. And I won't make any business-related deals with your dad, only with you."

There, that should prove something to her.

Only, he also needed to prove he was in this for himself. He already knew Rusty enough to know she wouldn't trust altruistic reasons.

Will cleared his throat. "And when all is said and done, we arrange a business deal that benefits both ranches."

Rusty bit her lip and dropped her gaze to the dirt. "So, this would be what, a marriage in name only? And we'd end it after Dad—" She swallowed.

Denial kicked him hard in the solar plexus, but she'd run a country mile if he said he wanted a real marriage. "I assume we would need to remain married for a period of time after you inherit. And... I don't want to worry my family and friends, so we would need to make it look real."

That brought her gaze back up to his. "Are you serious?"

"As a preacher in church. Hopefully, after the initial shock wears off, during which we might need to convince a few people, we can just be friendly roommates."

"Roommates." She was starting to sound like a parrot. Shock? Or was she thinking it through?

"I looked it up. Wyoming doesn't have a waiting period. We could be married before we go back to Texas. Present your dad with the certificate before we go."

"Next up, folks." The boom of the announcer broke over them. "Barrel racing."

"Shit," Rusty hissed. Then she glared at him. "You

thought right before my final ride would be a good time to talk about this?" She walked on, towing a very confused Mischief in her wake.

He grimaced, but couldn't take it back. He could only go forward. "We get along."

She snorted.

"When you don't suspect me of siding with your father," he amended. "We both love what we do and could work together. And this arrangement could benefit us both in the end." He grabbed her by the elbow and swung her to face him. "Those are as good grounds as any for a solid partnership. Making your dad's last days... errr... happy and getting you your ranch while helping to grow my business justifies the means. Don't you think?"

Rusty only shook her head. "I can't do this right now."

"Just promise me you'll think about it."

A high, slightly off-kilter laugh burst from her. "Hard to think of anything else," she muttered.

He waited, staring her down.

"Fine. I'll think about it. Mind if I do my event now? I have several thousand dollars riding on this, you know."

"Okay."

She turned again and he followed.

Behind the scenes, Rusty stopped Mischief by where several other ladies were standing with their horses, or already mounted. As the current leader after the first two rounds, Rusty was slated to go last.

Expression one of total concentration, as though she'd blocked out their entire conversation with ease, she flipped a stirrup up over the saddle and checked the girth, tightening it.

Mischief gave a groan and Will patted his neck. "Stop being such an old man," he told the horse.

Mischief responded by leaning into Rusty who pushed right back then kept fiddling with the strap. "You big baby."

Mischief let loose a long sigh and shook his head. Horses all had a personality. Mischief lived up to his name.

"You do a good ride, and I promise a couple of carrots and even an apple will be waiting for you when we get back to the barn," Rusty said to the horse.

His ears flickered at the word apple. The goofball loved them.

Satisfied with her gear, Rusty gathered the reins and a hank of Mischief's mane, then glanced at Will. "Give me a leg up?"

He kept his surprise to himself. Up till now, she never asked for help. Will cupped his hands and she put her knee in it, then he lifted and she swung her other leg over the horse's back, settling in the saddle.

Together, they waited as the eleven other ladies made their run at the barrels, one at a time. Maggie, one of the first up, turned in a fantastic time, bringing her into the second-place spot overall.

He stayed quiet as they moved closer to Rusty's turn to

ride, knowing she needed to focus, something he'd already ruined, that she was probably trying to visualize her run. He kept a steady hand on Mischief's reins. The horse knew what was coming and was already starting to dance, feet shuffling as he pranced in place, as keyed up to go as his rider.

Will settled a hand on her thigh, meaning the gesture to be one of support, but immediately regretting it as the warm feel of her taut flesh under her jeans registered. "You ready?"

She glanced over the other women, not even acknowledging his hand, as though she hadn't even noticed his touch. "It's a tough group up for this short go. I've been up against most of them at one point or another." She shrugged. "Anyone's game."

Will nodded his understanding. "Ride it like I've seen you do, and let everything else go."

Was he just making it worse for her? The glance she sent him was unreadable, but he thought he recognized a connection, like she realized he got it, that he was only talking about the rodeo. They shared this somehow, were in on it together.

"Yes," she finally said.

Then it was all about the ride. They waited, Mischief's feet moving more and more, kicking up dust, and Rusty having to take in the reins to hold him steady, until it was their turn. As it came closer to her turn, Will let go of the horse, moving to the side to let Rusty do her thing. She hardly seemed to notice.

"Our final rider up is our time leader after the first two rounds. Rusty Walker and her horse, Mischief Maker, have only been working together a short time, but have already proved themselves to be a pair to contend with. Rusty hails to us from… well, this is new, folks. Rusty is usually with Rising Star Ranch out of Wyoming, but now claims home with High Hill Ranch out of Texas."

Damn, that sounded good. Like she was already his, even if the truth was so far from that wish.

Will was suddenly glad he'd warned Rusty about changing her info for the announcements. By the way her chin went up, he had a feeling if that had been a surprise to her, he could've thrown her off her game. Not that proposing to her twenty minutes before her ride hadn't already done that.

What the hell was I thinking?

The announcer continued. "Looks like Williams Hill snapped her up to train his barrel racers. Let's see what Rusty and Mischief Maker can do tonight, folks!"

The announcer finished his intro and with barely a flick of her heels, horse and rider took off like a whip had been cracked over them. Will found himself holding his breath as she rounded first one barrel, then another, up and around the third, and straight back to where he waited in the shadows. They flew so fast, Rusty's hat was coming off, and she put a hand up to yank it down as they blew past where he stood.

She pulled Mischief up sharply, the horse almost sitting

as he used his strong hind quarters to skid to a halt, throwing up dirt in his wake. Rusty stopped to listen for her time.

"And that's a new record at CFD, folks." The announcer came over the loudspeakers. "As well as putting Rusty in first place overall." The crowd went nuts, clapping and whistling.

Rusty punched her hand in the air, though the move had Mischief dancing to the side.

"Come back out here, Rusty," the announcer invited.

She wheeled the horse and entered the arena, waving to the crowd to acknowledge her accomplishment, her face lit with a smile that made her glow, and Will's heart stuttered at the sight.

Damn, she was gorgeous.

A sudden need to see her smile like that because of him gripped him. What would that be like?

Rusty, still grinning, trotted out of the arena. Spotting him, she directed Mischief his way. "Did you see?" she called.

Will laughed. "Hard to miss."

She stopped where he waited. In a burst of elation, she jumped off the back of the horse and threw her arms around Will in a hug. He hesitated only a fraction of a second before wrapping his arms around her and pulling her in tight. Lord, she smelled good—horses and strawberries and leather and hay.

She was practically vibrating in his arms. She pulled back, though she didn't drop her arms. "That was amazing."

Her red ponytail swung as she shook her head, dark eyes glittering.

You were amazing. "Yes, it was," he limited himself to saying.

She laughed, and again his heart tripped up, bouncing around inside his chest. "The horse had something to do with it," she said.

"Marry me." Damn. He'd gone and done it again. "Let's partner up. I know it'll work."

Instead of frowning, Rusty quieted in his arms. "You mean it?"

He quirked his lips in a half smile. "I've asked you twice, already."

She closed her eyes and shook her head, and seemed to hold her breath.

"Rusty?" he prodded.

"Yes." She opened her eyes and blinked like she was surprised at herself.

Will searched her expression. "Yes, you'll marry me?"

She nodded. "I guess we're both crazy."

What would she do if he kissed her right now?

"That was a good ride."

Rusty froze in his arms at the sound of the male voice behind her. Will glanced up to find Garrett Walker approaching them, his leathery face set in his customary brooding expression.

A glance down showed every spark of happiness and

shock and whatever else had been staring him in the face seconds ago had been sucked out of the woman he still held. Instead of vibrating with exhilaration, Rusty tensed beneath his hands. She seemed to school her features before turning, and Will reluctantly let her go, dropping his arms to his sides.

"Thanks, Dad," she said.

"So..." Garrett flicked a glance between them before zeroing in on Rusty. "You're working for High Hill Ranch now?"

"Yes." A wealth of emotion in that one word, at least as far as Will was concerned. Too much for him to pinpoint exact ones.

"You know what that means," Garrett said.

Will frowned, his hands tightening on her hips. Was that a threat?

"Actually, Dad, you can congratulate us." Rusty slipped her hand into Will's, and he was shocked to find her trembling. He tightened his grip, trying to give her support through that physical connection.

She took a deep breath. "Will and I just got engaged."

Chapter Seven

THIS WAS HANDS down the dumbest thing she'd ever done in her life. She was marrying a man she hardly knew—a good man who didn't deserve to be mixed up in this, just to thwart her dad. Meanwhile, her father appeared to be in hog heaven.

Well, not at first. At first, he'd looked at her cockeyed, spat on the ground, and declared the engagement bullshit.

But Will'd taken offense to that. "We're getting married at the justice of the peace tomorrow, sir. And Rusty's coming home with me."

Home. With Will. That sounded way too good.

Still, the words had taken some of the wind out of dear old Dad's sails. Not to mention stealing some breath from her own lungs. She'd stood beside Will undaunted. A united front.

To which her father had declared he'd give the bride away himself.

Dammit.

Not only that, he'd insisted on more than a "hole-in-the-wall affair" as he put it. Her father, the stingiest man alive, had insisted on bringing Doris, their housekeeper who'd practically raised Rusty, down to help Rusty find an appropriate dress, as well as ponying up for a reception.

She'd protested.

He'd insisted.

Will and Rusty had given in, eventually. He'd decided not to invite his family as they'd all have to fly up at short notice, and not having enough time to get their large extended family there too. Instead, he'd asked that they do another short ceremony and reception in Texas for them. A reason her father seemed to swallow.

Now, here she stood, hair curled and the sides pinned back from her face, makeup perfect, and a gorgeous dress. Her father had insisted, and fate had decided to step in and lend an unwanted hand, because she'd found the perfect one.

Pink. Strapless and floor length with layered organza in white with pale pink flowers pattered on some of the layers. It had an empire waist. The top crisscrossed her breasts, making her look more buxom than she was thanks to the sweetheart neckline.

Guess all those years shoving the fact that I was a woman down Dad's throat paid off. Even she had to admit she'd never felt lovelier.

She stared at her reflection in the mirror in the bathroom at the justice of the peace, where she'd insisted on getting ready, and did her best not to cry. Though Doris would think them happy tears. In actual fact, her heart ached with the knowledge this *should* be her wedding dress, worn on the day she walked down the aisle to a man she loved.

Not this… sham.

"You look so beautiful." Doris sniffled behind her. Then she frowned. "Are you sure—"

"I'm sure." Rusty even tried a smile.

Poor Doris, mother hen that she'd always been, didn't believe Rusty wasn't doing this for the reasons she was. The woman was too keen and knew Rusty too well. She'd been asking that over and over since she got here to help get things ready for the wedding and reception.

"Huh." Doris grunted. "I guess if a man looked at me the way Will looks at you, I'd be pretty sure too."

Rusty spun around to face her. "Oh? And how does he look at me?"

Doris gave one of her no-nonsense frowns. "You know how, young lady."

"Nope. Tell me."

That earned her an eye roll. "Like he wants to spend all day in bed with you." She gave Rusty's behind a swat, shooing her out of the door. "Don't keep him waiting."

Did he look at her that way? They'd kissed, and she'd certainly been aware of… something… a tension between them.

But that didn't mean he felt it too. He was in this for what it would bring him in the end—a solid partnership with one of the biggest rodeo stock providers in the country.

Just good business. An odd way to go about it, granted, but that was all she was to Will. Just like every other man in her life, this had nothing to do with her as a person for him. Even if he was nice about it.

Outside the judge's chambers, she found her father standing in the hallway, tugging at his bow tie. An actual bow tie and a suit. The man must've lost his mind.

"Can't stand these contraptions," he muttered.

"You're the one who wanted a fancy wedding," she pointed out.

He didn't respond, merely shoved a bouquet at her. She flicked a glance at his stalwart face before taking it.

The flowers were gorgeous. Pink peonies and roses mixed with white narcissus and pearl-centered stephanotis. "Thank you, Dad," she murmured softly.

He shoved his hands in his suit pockets. "They're not from me."

Of course they weren't. She'd been an idiot to think they might be. Why she allowed the fission of disappointment any room inside her heart, she'd never know.

"Doris?" she asked.

"No. They're from your groom."

Disappointment abated in the face of something lighter, sweeter. Scarier.

Will had thought to provide her a wedding bouquet? And, by the looks of the flowers, had picked them out himself. Or at least told the florist that pink needed to be involved. She tried to trap a smile behind her lips, but failed.

"Better not keep the man waiting," her father grumbled now.

To her surprise, he offered her his arm. She took it and stared up at him a long moment, searching his familiar, craggy face.

He opened his mouth, as though something nice or kind might come out of it, but only closed it and reached for the door handle.

Again, disappointment seeped through her. But then she stepped forward, and her gaze went inexorably to the man standing in front of the judge's bench. A man who was marrying her because he was that kind of guy.

Yes, they had a deal. But Williams Hill wasn't the type to do something this big just for himself. Some part of her knew, without a doubt, this was for her.

And she had no idea how she felt about that.

Will—all fancy in a rented gray suit—turned from the judge to face her, and stilled.

Oh God. What's he thinking? Is he going to run?

Then he smiled—his handsome face with the sexy cleft chin and crooked nose somehow familiar to her in a way that made her heart stutter—and her soul settled. He was sticking this out. For better or worse, they were in this thing together.

Her father handed her over to Will, and Rusty had to laugh. She reached out and tweaked his tie. "Pink?"

He grinned. "Turned out to be a wise choice." He

glanced down at her dress.

She giggled. Nervous laughter, but that was okay. Nerves were normal for any bride. No one would be the wiser.

"You ready?" Will murmured.

She looked into his incredible blue eyes. Steady blue eyes that reflected back only easy confidence in the crazy thing they were about to do.

Rusty nodded. "Yes."

With a nod, Will turned to the judge who waited, smiling. "We're ready, sir."

The rest of the short, sweet ceremony passed in a bit of a blur. Rusty assumed she said and did everything right, because suddenly there was a solid platinum ring on her finger and the judge was pronouncing that Will could kiss his bride.

She hadn't thought about that bit. But the quick moment of panic melted away as Will took her face between his hands and claimed her lips in the sweetest kiss—warm, and beautiful, and hot. She wanted to lean into him, and just float away.

Forget the others.

Forget the deal.

Forget this wasn't even reality.

But he broke it off, blue eyes twinkling at her. Had he guessed how affected she'd been? That would be embarrassing.

"Ladies and gentleman," the judge announced, "I present

to you, Mr. and Mrs. Williams and Ruth Hill."

Blinking to clear her hazy mind, Rusty hooked her arm through Will's—or did he do that for her—and reached for her bouquet which Doris held. They walked out of the chamber, followed by her father, Doris, the hands, and a few friends of the family her father had invited who'd been able to come at short notice.

I'm married. I married Will.

Reception time. Ugh.

Doris had managed to find a hotel with a small reception room not already booked, and able to accommodate a party their size with one day's notice.

Hours of pinning a fake smile to her lips and pretending to be madly in love—because why else would she be marrying this hastily—for an audience that included the most mistrustful man on the planet. Sure he was happy she was getting married, but no doubt he already suspected her of doing so just to get her inheritance. His Machiavellian mind had to be spinning with ways to manipulate the situation further. Any sign of weakness or doubt between her and Will would be exploited.

Good times.

Will bustled her into the cab of his truck, which he'd obviously had detailed because it sparkled inside and out and smelled of leather oil. Guilt piled on. He was doing way too much for her with all this.

As soon as he pulled away, he glanced at her. "Am I allowed to tell you how beautiful you look?"

She scrunched up her nose. "Better not. I'll think you mean it."

"I do."

Her heart did a fair imitation of a bucking bronco at the words and the way his voice went all gruff.

Rusty cleared her throat and gave her heart stern instructions to quit that immediately. "Please don't. We shouldn't muddy the waters with…" She looked out her window, shaking her head.

He reached down and squeezed her hand, which rested on the console between them. "I get it. No messy emotions."

She blew out a relieved breath. "Exactly."

He nodded, and released her hand, which, contrarily, she didn't want him to do. "We might have to keep up the charade for the reception."

"True. But we'll know that's all for show."

Yup. All for show. They were on the same page. She should be relieved. So why was she facing a weird kind of disappointment?

He pulled up outside the hotel where her father had arranged a private room for their reception. "Ready?" Will asked.

She leaned over to look out his window and scrunched up her face. "Guess we'd better get this over with."

Get it over with was right.

He and Rusty paused in the hallway outside the Lovebird suite. Inside the small room, the twenty-five-or-so folks who'd been in the judge's chambers gathered. Several larger tables with white cloths, set for a sit-down meal, were spaced around the room. And a DJ was set up in the corner playing soft music.

"Your dad went all out," he said.

"Uh-huh." The dubious note to her voice made him wonder at her thoughts.

Will eyed a single, round table intimately set for two situated at the front of the room. "Looks like they reserved us some seating," he murmured.

Rusty gave a soft snort. "On the downside, we'll be stared at while we eat. But on the plus side, we won't have to talk to anyone."

Will grinned. "You're all silver linings today. Guess we'd better practice our goo-goo eyes."

She tilted her chin at a haughty angle. "I don't goo-goo."

Will heaved an exaggerated sigh. "So I'll be goo-gooing all by myself? What'll people think?"

"You married me after knowing me a handful of weeks. I'd say they already have an idea that you've lost your mind."

"Or found the perfect woman." The second the words left his mouth he wanted to pull them back in. Because that was something a real groom would say, and damned if he knew what he was. But a real groom wasn't it.

"Will your family be upset that they missed all this?" she asked.

"We'll probably have to set up a similar run through when we get back to Texas. Mom will feel better when we tell her your dad surprised us with it."

She tipped her chin to eye him. "You'd lie to them?"

"It's not entirely a lie. He may have given us a day or two to get stuff set up, but it was still a surprise."

She shook her head. "I took you for one of those Boy Scout, never-tell-a-lie types."

"The Aggie motto. Never lie, cheat, or steal," he said.

"Hmmm... just elaborate, collaborate, and borrow. Right?"

Will tipped his head back and laughed. "Where'd you pick that up?"

"I lived with Garrett Walker," came the dry answer.

But Will's laughter had brought notice from their guests. At some unseen signal, the DJ suddenly hushed the sound and came over the speakers. "Introducing the bride and groom. Mr. and Mrs. Will and Rusty Hill."

They were bustled into the room and Will shook hands and received hugs and kisses on his cheek as Rusty was separated from him to do the same.

One of the first to shake his hand was Garrett Walker. "You're a good man, Son. Proud to have you in the family."

"Thanks." What else could he say to that? Something like, *how the hell would you know*, probably wouldn't look good right at this moment.

Garrett tightened his grip, pulling Will in closer. "I expect a baby announcement from the two of you before the year is out, of course."

Shock fried Will's ability to speak. Did her dad just say that? He had to mean it as a thing people said at weddings, right? Before Will could open his mouth, Walker clapped him on the back. "Let's enjoy the party."

For a guy supposedly fighting serious illness, his new father-in-law certainly seemed optimistic that he'd still be around. Will gave himself a mental smack. Rusty's suspicions when it came to her father were starting to color his own opinion. He should give the man the benefit of the doubt. For now.

Will was passed onto another friend of the Walkers, then another, and then another. Meanwhile, he couldn't keep his eyes off Rusty, who was ahead of him moving through the room.

His bride was stunning. He'd almost laughed when the doors to the chamber had opened to reveal her there in a softly pink dress.

He'd got the flowers right, at least, and his tie.

But mostly, he'd had to force himself to remember how to breathe, because she was about the most gorgeous thing he'd ever seen. All her gloriously red hair curled and pulled away from her face, and the feminine gown floating around her body. And the way she'd looked at him—like he was her anchor in a stormy sea.

"He's a better man than I am, taking her on," one of Garrett's hands muttered.

But Will overheard it. He clenched his jaw around a smile as he talked to a little old lady who was a neighbor of the Walkers, but what he really wanted to do was clock the guy.

Instead, as soon as he'd finished polite chatting Mrs. Stephens, he turned around. "I *must be* a better man than you, because she's amazing." He paused, satisfied at how the other man's mouth dropped open before he scowled. "Actually," Will continued. "What I am is damn lucky she picked me."

With that, he turned on his bootheel and walked over to where Rusty already waited at their table. She watched him approach, her expression giving nothing away, but as soon as he was close, she stepped into him, taking his face between her hands, and laid a sweet, soft kiss against his lips. Paused, and kissed him again.

Then drew back and smiled at what he was sure was an idiotically dumbfounded expression plastered across his face. "You're a good man, Williams Hill."

He grinned. "I agree. But what made you decide I deserved a kiss for it?"

She shrugged. "I heard."

Damn. He thought he'd kept that encounter quiet, not wanting to embarrass her. "Sorry."

She shook her head as he held out her chair for her.

"Don't be. I've been dealing with that ass for years. Nice to finally have some backup."

Rusty did not lower her voice, and Will grinned as a twitter buzzed through the room. Yup. Amazing.

They managed to make it through the meal in relative peace, only being called upon to kiss a few times. Thankfully, Rusty had talked her dad out of most of the traditions, so there was no dancing, no cake cutting, and no official speeches.

That was, until Mrs. Stephens heard about it. "No dancing?!" she exclaimed loud enough for everyone to stop eating. "But they have to share a dance at least."

"Oh, Lord," Rusty whispered. "She won't quit until we do."

"Guess, we'd better then," Will whispered back.

Rusty's eyes widened as he stood up from the table and crossed to the DJ to make a request, then approached where she still sat, watching him.

Will held out a hand. "May I have this dance, Mrs. Hill?"

Something vulnerable flashed in her eyes as the soft strains of "Feels Like Home," the Linda Ronstadt version, came over the speakers. But she put her hand in his, and stood as he wrapped his other hand around her waist. Then he moved them into a slow two-step, their bodies moving in time to the music as if they'd been dancing together like this for years. Not a single trip or damaged toe.

A miracle as far as he was concerned. Women among his family and friends avoided dancing with him for a reason. But Rusty moved with him, and Will forgot to be worried about it, focusing instead on her upturned face.

Rusty stared up at him, her expression unreadable, as they danced, and Will didn't look away. He didn't want to break the moment, the… something… between them that was real. Could she feel it too?

Finally, the song ended, and he leaned down, kissing her lush lips that pulled him like gravity until he crashed into her.

They broke apart to the sound of clapping. "See." Mrs. Stephen's could be loudly heard declaring. "Every bride and groom need a dance. Makes it official."

Rusty grinned up at him—the first real smile she'd shown since the moment they'd announced to her father that they were engaged. "I guess we're official."

Chapter Eight

Dust kicked up behind Will's truck as Rusty followed him down the long gravel drive, obscuring her view of the buildings ahead. Two days of driving, two days by herself in the truck with her thoughts.

She had married Williams Hill.

Reality still hadn't sunk in.

They'd stayed the night in the honeymoon suite at the hotel where the reception had been held, again, her father's "treat."

As they'd thanked everyone for coming, Doris had yanked Rusty up against her generous bosom. "No thanks necessary, darlin'. Your father thought you'd like me to be here."

Even now, Rusty was stunned by that one act that seemed almost human. Damn her father and his stubborn pride, bullying her into doing exactly as he wanted. Only, thanks to the man in the truck in front of her, she'd beat her father at his own game.

At least they were finally here. High Hill Ranch.

Rusty hadn't spent much time in Texas. In fact, she'd

met Holly in Colorado to pick up Mischief. While she and Will drove south, she'd found the change in topography fascinating. The high plains of the panhandle had morphed into cotton crops followed by acres of short cedar trees and massive windmill farms, and finally the rolling hills covered with green-leafed live oaks among cedars and cactus.

Every so often they passed through small towns, some in better shape than others, but seeing them had made Rusty relax a tad. This wasn't so different from her home in Wyoming. Good, down-to-earth people lived here, and she'd be one of them.

As Will's wife.

Oh, God, what have I done?

For the thousandth time since she'd said "yes," Rusty gave herself a mental shake. She could do this. She could upheave her life and change everything about the course of her future in a fake marriage to a man who wanted to be business partners. All for the best in the end, she hoped.

Finally, she got a look at the main house. Like many homes in Texas she'd passed on the drive, the house was single story—ranch style, spreading out on each side from the double doors in the center. Built of white limestone that showed its age by some spots that had turned black, it had been well cared for over the years.

The house was surrounded by a well-tended lawn and she'd bet money a large garden lurked somewhere near, probably around back. She especially loved the tin roof and wrap-around covered porch with randomly grouped rocking chairs. She could imagine watching a thunderstorm gather from those chairs, iced tea on the table beside her.

Maybe even sweet iced tea. She'd never tried it, but, given her serious sweet tooth, would bet she'd like it.

Forget iced tea. She would be living in the main house. With her husband.

When she should be sharing the bunkhouse with the other hands. If she let herself think about it too much, she would run away right now and ask for an annulment. Especially knowing she was about to meet her in-laws.

Temporary though they might be.

Will bypassed the house and drove to the barn, and Rusty followed. Chris and Jordan, Will's rodeo hands were two days behind them as they had another rodeo to hit in New Mexico on the way home, but Will had wanted to return immediately and share their "good news" with his family before rumors reached them.

Rusty was inside the trailer, carefully backing out Mischief, who was a lamb when it came to travel, when she heard a female voice calling Will's name.

"Hi, Mom," he called back.

Oh, Lord.

Rusty scrunched up her face as she peeked around Mischief's bulk to Will's dark head outside. His face was turned away, as he looked at his mother in the distance. She was going to meet his mother now? She wouldn't have minded a shower and a chance to freshen up first. Rodeo had always meant a lot of travel, and usually the last thing she wanted at the end of a two-day drive was having to put on her social face and be nice to total strangers. But this was so much more, so much worse.

In-laws, not strangers.

People she'd be living and working with day in and day out for a while. Except when they went to Rising Star. While her father's manipulations meant she couldn't live with him all the time these last months, he was still her father and he was dying. Will had agreed they'd split their time between the two ranches as much as possible.

Her new husband turned back to face her and caught her gaze. He waved her to continue. With pressure on the lead, Rusty backed the horse out, the clomp of hooves against the trailer floor echoing around her.

Outside, she blinked in the bright sunlight for a second, and appreciated the breeze. July in Texas was miserably hot, at least today it was, but even worse in that trailer, despite how it was vented for air, which helped when on the road, but not as much when stopped.

"Take Mischief inside and get him settled," Will said. "His stall is third on the right. You can meet the family when you're done. Just come on up to the house."

Her expression must've said how much she relished that idea. He was going to abandon her to walk in there alone?

To her shock, Will lowered his head to plant a quick kiss

on her unsuspecting lips. "It'll be fine, Rusty. I want to tell them first so that you don't have to deal with the shocked part of their reaction. Don't worry—" He squeezed her hand. "They'll love you."

Still shaken from the brief kiss and the confidence in his gaze, Rusty didn't argue, turning immediately for the shade of the barn. And, yes, she might've spent more time caring for the horse than was strictly necessary.

She even made a quick call. Except a gruff male voice answered the phone. "Dad?" she asked.

"Yeah."

No way was her father home in the middle of the afternoon without good reason. "You feeling okay?"

"No. I'm not okay. I'm dying. But not today, so don't worry about it."

In other words, don't show any concern at risk of irritating the tar out of him. But if anything was proof that her father truly was sick, his being at home at this time, after two days "off" dealing with her marriage.

"I just called to let Doris know we made it back to the ranch okay." Because her father sure as hell never asked.

"I'll tell her you called."

"Thanks, Dad. I'll—"

The click on the other end told her he'd hung up. He never had been one for wasting time with pleasantries like hellos or goodbyes.

Rusty gazed toward the house where her new in-laws

awaited. Washing up would've been nice. A glance behind her showed a sink, so she used that to rinse off her hands and face, wiping the sweat from the back of her neck.

Wyoming had its own form of intense summer heat, but nothing like this oppressiveness. The air was stifling, weighing down on her like a physical presence. A shower was going to feel like heaven. But first, time to meet the family.

The closest door to the barn she could see was the front door. She hesitated. Did she ring the doorbell? Or did she go around back and let herself in? The hands on her ranch used the back door, but she wasn't a hand. She also hadn't been introduced yet.

With a sigh, she turned her boots for the front door. Before she rang the doorbell, she took off her boots and deposited them by the front door.

She was about to ring a second time, worried no one had heard her, when the red door was swung open by Will.

He didn't look upset. In fact, when he saw her face, he chuckled. "Don't look so worried. They're all excited to meet you."

"I'll bet," she muttered.

"Come on. Pretend you're ripping off a bandage."

He took her by the hand, his touch only marginally helping the nerves growing tentacles inside her stomach. Rusty made a noncommittal sound as she allowed him to lead her through a living room and down a long hallway, the vague sounds of voices floating back to them.

Rusty stopped at the door, and tried not to visibly swallow as she took in the scene. *Oh, God. The entire Hill tribe has been gathered.*

Could've used a warning about that. Did they always greet each other like this when they'd been out of town? Will'd only been gone a few weeks. Her father had never bothered to meet her at the door when she arrived after a trip. Hell, often he wasn't even at home, usually out doing his chores or dealing with business, often at other rodeos.

Will put his hand at the small of her back to usher her in. Or push her in. Not much difference at this point.

The first person she came to as they walked farther into the kitchen was a petite woman with dark hair cut in a short bob that curled just under her ears. Only the lines fanning out from the corners of her eyes gave any indication of her age.

"You must be, Rusty," the other woman said in a thick Texas drawl. "Will told us the news."

This had to be his mother. Was she happy? She didn't look like she'd been crying or anything.

"Come on in, darlin'." She was beckoned to come closer. "We don't stand on ceremony around here and you're family now."

As soon as Rusty stepped closer, she was pulled into a big hug from a very tiny woman. "We couldn't be happier that Will finally found someone."

Finally?

The room erupted in talk and congrats. Rusty had no idea what she'd been expecting—everything from tears and recriminations to disappointment—but not this.

"You are so beautiful. I can see why he fell for you so quickly," his mother said. "And you love horses as much as he does. Perfect."

Will had certainly said a lot in the time she'd been handling Mischief. Too much, maybe. He'd laid it on too thick. They would either not believe their instalove story, or they'd be so disappointed when they split it would be awful.

"We can't wait to watch the video," Will's mom continued.

Video? Uh-oh.

"We can watch it after dinner, Mom," Will said.

Wait. What? She swung her gaze to his, trying not to let the others see her panic.

He caught her confused expression. "I had one of the hands use my phone to record the ceremony and part of the reception."

He did?

Suddenly the enormity of what she and Will were doing—lying to his family and her father so she could keep her ranch—struck with all the weight of a sledgehammer. Her father was one thing; he'd forced her hand. But Will's family... She could already tell these were lovely people.

Will's mom backed up, tears in her eyes, and smiled. "I'm forgetting my manners. We haven't even been introduced. I'm Will's mom, Evaline Hill."

Rusty chuckled and smiled back. Hard not to when such open kindness was directed her way. "I figured. Nice to meet you, Mrs. Hill."

"Evaline, please."

Will stepped up behind her and wrapped an arm around her waist. Rusty sucked in a sharp breath at the contact.

"Relax," he whispered in her ear. Louder he said, "Let me introduce you to everyone else."

He turned her to face the others. "You know Holly, who I will forever be grateful to for finding you."

She pinched his arm, and he jerked slightly under her fingers. But hopefully he got the message. *Too much, Will.*

A familiar woman with dark wavy hair almost to her waist and wearing a gypsy-ish skirt in greens and purples moved forward. Like Evaline just had, Holly Hill pulled Rusty into a hug. At least Will had to let go of her. "Nice to see you again. And with such happy news! When I suggested you hire on here, I sort of hoped Will might make a move."

Rusty choked on that one, and tried to hide her snort with a chuckle. "I'm sure you're all shocked. It happened… sort of fast."

Before Holly pulled away, she whispered in Rusty's ear, "Don't let the large family thing intimidate you. They're harmless and thrilled."

Dang. Had her nerves been that obvious?

Will twined his fingers through hers and tugged her to

the next person, a man who the Hill kids had obviously taken after. "This is my father."

"You can call me John." The older version of Will also gathered her in for a quick hug, before releasing her back into Will's care.

Same dark hair, though graying at the temples, and same startling blue eyes, not remotely dimmed by time, which gazed back at her now. She got a good idea of what Will would look like in his fifties—attractive, that was for dang sure. She flicked a glance up at him, mentally picturing it. Of all the Hills, each of whom was tall except Evaline, Will was the tallest.

"I knew when Will finally found the right woman for him, he wouldn't wait around," John said. "He always was one to go after what he wanted."

Except Will didn't want her—not as a wife. He wanted a business partner. A horrible feeling settled in the center of her chest—rocks piled on rocks piled on nausea. What had she done to him?

"Holly is married to my brother Cash," Will continued the introductions.

An only slightly shorter, less lanky version of Will, dressed in the browns and tans of a Texas sheriff, also gave her a hug. "Welcome to the family."

"Me next!" A tiny blonde peanut of a girl jumped up and down next to Cash, hardly able to contain her excitement.

Rusty dropped to her level with a smile. "And you are?"

The girl, who had to be around six, drew herself up tall. "I am Sophia Ivy Hill. This is my daddy, and Holly is my new mama."

"That must make you pretty special."

"Where are your mom and dad?"

Rusty flicked a glance at Will, but his expression gave nothing away. "My dad lives in Wyoming where I grew up. My mom passed away a long time ago."

Solemn Hill-blue eyes regarded her for a long moment, then Sophia threw her arms around Rusty's neck. "My mama died too, and so did Holly's. But it's okay, because they watch over us from heaven."

Rusty had to fight hard to keep her stinging eyes from spilling over the sweet child's sincere need to make her feel better. "Yes, they are."

Sophia drew back to study Rusty's face. "You have sad eyes." Rusty froze. How did one handle a comment like that in front of her pseudo-family?

Before she could say anything, Sophia looked over her shoulder. "You should fix that Uncle Will."

Holy smokes. Awkward did not begin to cover this moment.

"Okay, munchkin," Cash said. "Rusty still needs to meet the rest of the family."

Sophia's arms tightened around her for a second before she released Rusty who ruffled Sophia's hair before she got to her feet. She looked at the only person she could without it being really weird. Will.

He took her hand again, turning her to two other men. "These runts are Jennings and Autry." Two younger versions of the older brothers, in their early to mid-twenties, nodded and grinned.

Rusty took a deep breath, thankful everyone had let that moment pass.

"I wouldn't exactly call them runts," she murmured. They were well over six feet. The younger brothers both winked at her in unison and she chuckled. Did they do that all the time?

"Carter is away at school right now," Will said. "But you'll meet her as soon as her summer session is over, sometime in August before fall semester starts up."

Right. Rusty slapped a smile she hoped was suitably friendly on her face, because, by now, she was feeling a jumble of emotions—panic, guilt, and misgivings layered with the strangest feeling of comfort. Like she'd known these folks longer than minutes. "It's very nice to meet you all. I'm sure our news has been a surprise, and I'm sorry that we married without you there to see it."

"Don't you worry about that," John said. "Will explained about your dad being sick, and rushing it for him. We're so sorry, honey."

"Oh..." The word came out faintly.

"You're part of the family now," Evaline added. "And maybe we can arrange a reception in the next month or two to celebrate with friends here."

Oh, hell. Will had warned her, and she couldn't deny them that at the least. "That sounds lovely," she said. Did her voice sound as faint as she thought?

"We'd love that, Mom," Will added. "Plus, I'd love to see Rusty in her wedding dress again."

He slipped an arm around her, and she gained some strength from his touch, taking a deep breath. She wasn't in this alone. She hadn't tricked him into this situation, he'd suggested it. She could do this. They could do this.

A glance up showed him watching her closely. His blue eyes steady, maybe even amused. She tried to keep from frowning in front of his family. What did he have to be amused about anyway?

"Are you hungry?" Evaline asked. "Will's always starved after a long trip."

"Maybe because he doesn't stop except for gas or to take care of the horses," Rusty commented wryly.

Will shrugged, unperturbed, and everyone around her laughed.

"He gets it from his father, I'm afraid." Evaline rolled her eyes. "I'd stop at every Cracker Barrell between here and Cheyenne if the men in my life let me."

"The chicken and dumplings are the best," Rusty agreed, flicking a glance at Will. She was starting to feel like she'd entered an alternate universe. They'd just found out Will was married and they were talking chicken and dumplings?

"What do you want on your sandwich, Rusty?" Evaline asked.

"Oh, I'm not—"

Rusty's protest was cut off as Will ushered her to one of the stools situated around the island in the kitchen. Noise filled the room as the Hills busied themselves making lunch and grabbing seats either at the island or at the kitchenette table to Rusty's right.

Evaline looked up at her with eyebrows raised in question. "Dear?"

"Oh, um… ham with cheese and mustard?"

Will's mom smiled. "Coming right up."

"I'll have the same, Mom," Will said from his seat beside her.

He pulled her stool closer to his so she sat between the "V" of his legs. Part of her wanted to lean into him, feeling oddly protected. The other part, the part that was almost vibrating with tension, wanted some space.

She leaned in and kissed his cheek, aware of the subtle tension that gripped his body, then whispered in his ear, "Don't lay it on too thick."

As she pulled back, he caught her chin in his hands and kissed her. Not a brief peck, but a claiming kiss that went on too long, given their audience, but still managed to short-circuit her mind until she leaned into him.

He pulled back and kissed the tip of her nose. "I know what I'm doing," he whispered.

Did he? Because she'd lost her way entirely. Damn that man could kiss.

Evaline cleared her throat, but Rusty didn't miss his mother's glowing smile. She pointed a mustard covered knife at him. "You can get your own, young man. Rusty's your bride and a guest, at least for today."

"Yes, ma'am." Will hopped up and circled the counter to get started on his sandwich.

In short order, Rusty had a heaping sandwich in front of her, along with chips, potato salad, fresh strawberries, and a pickle spear. Usually, she ate whatever Doris made the night before. And, more often than not, her meals were taken alone. This was a far cry from her usual.

The Hills chatted around her as they ate, tossing questions her way like a barrage as they tried to get to know Will's new wife.

She was his wife. What had she got herself into?

They seemed to share everything. First they wanted to know all about how Will and Rusty met. They'd agreed beforehand to stick to the truth as much as possible, leaving out the part about her father's ultimatum. After that, they talked about the wedding, then the rodeos. Then Cash shared a funny story about a recent arrest. Holly gave an update on the vet clinic where she worked. And then they got talking ranch business.

And every second, Rusty was horribly, uncomfortably aware of how Will's thigh was pressed against hers under the countertop. He'd resumed his seat around her. She'd tried to scoot over to make room for Autry, but his mother was on her left, and already bumping elbows.

Besides, Will clearly had a plan in mind about how they'd act, and she had no choice but to follow his lead. Newlyweds touched all the time. Right?

"So, Rusty," Evaline said. "That's an unusual name for a girl. Is there a story behind it?"

Will rolled his eyes. "Because we have stories behind our names—"

"And so do I," Holly interrupted.

He grinned at his sister-in-law. "And Holly, too. Mom thinks everyone must."

Rusty gave a dry chuckle. "Well, this time she would be right."

"Oh?" Will angled his head to look at her, eyes twinkling like they were sharing a personal moment, though his entire family surrounded them.

With effort, she pulled her gaze away from him to swing around and answer Evaline. "My first name is actually Ruth, and, as a baby, they called my Ruthie. But my brother, who was seven when I was born, had a bit of a lisp and couldn't say it. It always came out as Rusty, and eventually the name stuck." She flicked a hand, indicating her red braid. "Especially as it seemed so appropriate."

Autry chuckled. "Ruthie. That's cute. Mind if I call you that?"

She'd always thought of that as her brother's nickname for her, but somehow, Rusty didn't mind. "No."

Evaline sighed. "What a sweet story. What does your brother do now?"

Rusty always hated that question. Not for herself. She'd had a long time to come to terms with her brother's early passing. But for the person asking, she hated that they felt bad for asking when they learned.

"Reed passed away when Rusty was eleven, Mom," Will said quietly when Rusty hesitated.

Immediately, Evaline wrapped her closest arm around Rusty's shoulders. "Oh, sweetie. I am so sorry. I couldn't imagine. Your poor parents."

Rusty sent the woman an appreciative smile and had to resist the urge to snuggle into the motherly sympathy. "My mother died in childbirth with me, sadly. I never knew her. After Reed…" She shrugged. "It's been just Dad and me ever since."

And soon, just her. The impact of that thought, and how alone she suddenly felt, had her frowning.

"I don't have to call you that," Autry offered. "I wouldn't want to make you feel—"

She shook her head, pulling herself back into the conversation with effort. "No, really. I kind of missed it."

Will's brother, a younger version of him, grinned and sent her a wink. "Yes, ma'am."

Whatever force of gravity had her turning her head back

to face Will, she encountered his blue-eyed gaze on her and every part of her came to a screeching halt. His expression wasn't one of overt sympathy, but more one of understanding, like he saw the lonely little girl she'd been. One who'd had to keep up with the boys to prove herself. Though Doris had tried to show her how to be a girl, too. One whose father blamed her for her mother's death, and both rejected her and did his damndest to control everything about her life when his only son was stolen from him too soon.

"Now you have me," he mouthed, keeping the moment between the two of them, even though Evaline still hugged Rusty's shoulders.

For now. She bit her lip and gave a jerky little nod, playing the part even while her heart desperately wished he'd meant that.

Rusty straightened in her seat. If wishes were stars, she would've lit up the whole damn night sky by now. No use came from wishing.

Evaline gave her shoulder one more squeeze and let her go. "Well, we must seem like a loud, huge family all gathered together like this."

Rusty laughed. "It's very different from my home. That's for sure."

But she liked it. She was totally overwhelmed and out of her element, of course, but that would probably pass as she settled into her life here and got to know them.

A dull ache settled in her stomach, already knowing she'd

have to say goodbye to these good people. Probably sooner rather than later. Perhaps getting to know them wasn't a good idea. But unavoidable.

She held in a sigh. *What a mess.*

After lunch, which thankfully didn't involve any more questions directed at Rusty that made her too uncomfortable, Will took her by the hand. "Let's go get settled in."

Rusty's discomfort levels went off the charts. He'd slept on the couch in the honeymoon suite, and they'd got separate rooms at the places they stopped on the way home. But now, they had to play new lovers, and sleep in Will's room.

To keep her mind off that fact, she went for conversation around non-bedroom related logistics. "How are meals usually handled around here?"

Will paused in the long hallway that exited off the family room in the opposite direction from the kitchen. "Wait a second." He glanced over his shoulder, then back down at her. "I think we need to put on a little show," he whispered.

"What?" she asked.

But rather than answer, he pulled her into him and kissed her like he'd been thinking about it for days and couldn't wait a second longer. Despite the kiss they'd shared in the kitchen. Part of her felt like she was coming home, and the other part hated that fact. This was fake. A show for whoever Will thought was watching.

He sipped at her lips with soft yet urgent kisses, and no

matter how determined she was to not forget that this was fake, Rusty couldn't help but open to him when he ran his tongue along the seam of her lips.

A little sigh escaped her as he drew back. Will tucked a loose tendril of hair behind her ear. "I think we're in the clear now."

"Good." She straightened up and stepped away from him. "Do you think we'll have to do that often?"

He seemed to study her expression. Granted, she'd sounded edgy even to her own ears. "Just at first, probably," he said.

"Fine." She hid a wince. Now she sounded snotty.

"I'm not that bad a kisser, am I?" he teased.

No way was she touching that one with a ten-foot pole. She raised an eyebrow, and he laughed.

"Guess I'll have to work on my technique," he mused. The tilt to his lips indicated his continued amusement.

Heaven help her if he decided to do that with her. "Our room?" she asked, needing to get off the topic of kissing.

"WE'RE THIS WAY." Will started down a long, hallway with several doors leading to bedrooms.

Deliberately he turned his back on Rusty because she seemed to need him to stop staring, and, honestly, he needed to stop himself staring.

He'd married the gorgeous, stubborn woman, and he had no fucking clue how to go on from here. All he knew for sure was that he had a short period of time to convince her that this was real, to give them a chance, all without scaring her away. And touching her constantly, like he wanted, was definitely going to do that. No matter how he could justify those touches as a convincing show for his family. The show was for Rusty more than them. But her back was straight as a new iron fence post and her shoulders were up around her ears. He needed to back off.

Will opened the door at the far end and stood back so she could precede him inside.

She glanced around, taking in the queen-sized bed with its basic gray comforter which butted up against a wall of reclaimed barn wood that Will had installed himself. Heavy rustic furniture and a navy armchair by the window completed the room.

"Cozy," she murmured.

"Thanks. Feel free to spruce it up and make it yours."

She flicked a glance his way. One he had no trouble interpreting. She didn't like that idea at all. In Rusty's head, this was still a temporary arrangement.

"While you're here." He tacked on as though he hadn't noticed the glance. "Extra sheets are in the cupboard in the bathroom." He pointed at the door leading to their own private bathroom. The house had been built with the plan that a large family of multiple generations would live here together. For the first time in his life, Will was thrilled that Carter's room stood between his and Cash's, and that the room across the hall was an office. Essentially, he and Rusty would have added privacy with that cushion of space between them and the rest of the family.

But he was jumping the gun.

"Off the kitchen is the laundry room. We're on septic here, so try to space out your wash days. I assume you'll do yours and I'll do mine."

"Sounds good."

She shifted from foot to foot.

"I'll clear some drawers for you and some space in the closet."

"Oh, you don't have to—"

Damn the woman was skittish. "You can't live out of a suitcase."

She scrunched up her nose. "I guess not."

Maybe jumping straight to business would help her relax. "I suggest we take today and maybe tomorrow to get you settled in, then we can get started with the horses."

Immediately, her shoulders dropped and her nod this time was more eager. "I'm looking forward to that."

He hid his satisfaction that he'd read her right. "Good."

What else could he talk about that was more business-y? "We do community-style breakfast, which Mom cooks and serves up at the house for the family and any hands who didn't make their own," he explained. "Lunches are up to you to scrounge for yourself, and the hands typically have dinner in the bunkhouse while we have a family dinner in the house."

"Okay." She nodded again. "I'd better start unloading and unpacking, I guess."

Will studied her expression. Did she want help? She was so self-contained, he often had difficulty reading her. Still, his mother would tan his hide if she found out his wife had unloaded her truck by herself.

"Let's get started." He tugged her wrist, but she pulled up.

"I don't need any help," she said.

"Mom would kill me if I didn't. You really want my death on your hands?" He tried a smile.

Only she didn't smile back. "I don't need you taking care of me."

She was so damned stubborn. Will hooked his thumbs in his back pockets to keep his hands occupied, otherwise him might grab her and try to kiss her into a better mood. "When you meet the other hands you can ask, but one of us—my brothers or Dad or me—helped all of them move in. Just being neighborly. And you're my wife, for all intents and purposes. Of course, I would help you."

She continued to eye him with frustration, lips pursed.

Will shook his head. "You don't have manners in Wyoming?" he teased.

She blew out a breath that ruffled the one tendril of hair

that had escaped her braid. "Of course we have manners. But your family are like the Cleavers. No one is that... neighborly."

He could think of many more neighborly things he'd like to be doing with her about now. The big bed at his back beckoned. Unloading her truck was not high on the list.

"We are," he insisted. Then reached out and tugged her wrist again. "Come on. I'm going into town in two hours. You should come so I can show you around and we can shop for any foods you like that we don't have in the house and anything else you might need. So, if you're going to be done unpacking by then, you'd better get hopping."

This time she didn't resist, following him out into the blazing heat. "Has anyone ever called you bossy and domineering?" she asked as they walked to her truck, still parked at the barn.

"Nope," he said cheerfully. "I'm considered the easygoing Hill around these parts."

She snorted as she climbed into her truck. "That's because you're subtle. They didn't know they'd been bossed."

He settled beside her on the seat and grinned. "Probably so."

Her nose twitched, reminding him of a bunny rabbit.

"You're awfully cute when you get riled." The words popped out of his mouth before he could throw a rope and pull them back.

At least he hadn't tacked on the other thought, that she

was awfully kissable too. He wanted to kiss the irritation out of her eyes, kiss her until she turned sweet, and easy in his arms, like she had in the hall until she'd remembered where she was and who she was kissing and why.

She started the truck and slammed it into gear. "I am *not* cute," she ground through her teeth.

Will smartly held in the chuckle that wanted to escape. She pulled the truck around to the back, sliding it into a spot close to the door to make unloading easier. An hour later, after working in comfortable silence, they had everything piled into his room.

As soon as he put down the last box, she stood up. "Thanks for the help," she said. "I'm sure you want to spend a little more time with Cash and Holly before they have to go."

Taking her not-so-subtle hint, he moved to the door, but paused before walking out it. "You've got an hour before I go into town."

She shook her head, her braid slipping from her shoulder to hang behind her back. "I'll go later."

He cocked his head, deliberately schooling his features to casual indifference. "Maybe another day. But it makes sense to share the gas, and I can show you where things are in town."

Her berry-ripe lips pursed as she considered his words. "Fine. See you in an hour." With that she ushered him out, closing the door behind him with a soft but definitive click.

Will stared at the door, hands on his hips and shook his head. Closed out of his own bedroom by his brand-new wife. Not exactly a good sign. He was asking for trouble, tangling with Rusty Walker Hill, but he was having too much fun to stop. Besides, he had a marriage certificate in his glove box that said she was legally his to have and to hold, and he intended that to last a hell of a lot longer than a few months, even if she didn't know it yet.

He just had to convince his stubborn, suspicious wife he was worth keeping around.

An hour later, he pulled his truck around to the front of the house and honked. He would've gone in to get her, and his mother would probably have a fit, but he had a feeling Rusty would be less edgy if he treated her like a buddy for a while. A minute or two later, Rusty came outside. It took everything he had not to get out and open the door for her, but keeping to the buddy idea, he stayed where he was as she hopped up beside him.

"So…" Rusty said after the first few miles of silence. "Does your whole family get together like that a lot?"

He flicked a glance to find her looking out the window, her expression inscrutable. "Yeah. We get together whenever we can. La Colina is a bit of a drive from the ranch, so we don't see Cash and Holly as much as we'd like. And with Carter in Austin, we only see her on school breaks. Although—" He smiled now. "She's been seeing a guy in town, so she's made the trip more often lately."

"What does she want to do with her degree?" Rusty asked.

Will shrugged. "According to Carter, there are a few options, but I suspect she'll end up with a law firm in Austin as one of their primary specialists. She started consulting for them during her master's work."

"That might cause issues with the rancher she's seeing," Rusty pointed out.

Will concentrated on turning onto the main road. "They'll figure it out if it's important to them," he said.

She turned to face him. "That doesn't sound very romantic," she commented.

He kept his eyes forward. "I guess not."

"What? You don't believe in true love?"

Now she was teasing him. Trying to get a rise out of him? He'd have to stay on his toes to keep up with her mercurial moods.

"I believe that people can love each other completely their whole lives. My parents have. But I also think people try to make something work when it obviously shouldn't. Marriage is hard enough without adding distance or different values or needs to it."

The entire time he was talking, Will was painfully aware of how his current situation belied his words. However, he also believed he and Rusty were... What? Meant to be? He'd never been a big believer in fate or soul mates. But here he was married to a woman who didn't love him, and determined to change that. They just had to get to know each other.

"Do you always have an answer for everything?" she asked, but at least laughter lingered in her voice, rather than irritation.

Will smiled. "Hardly." For example, he had no answer to the question that was Rusty Walker.

The smart answer was keep the relationship on a business partnership footing. The dumb answer was hard and currently pushing against the zipper of his jeans.

He was doing his best to walk the fine line between the two. Will had never been the impulsive one of the Hill family. He was methodical, even when he took risks. This thing with Rusty was anything but methodical. He was flying by the seat of his jeans.

"My experience is love, like any other vice—greed, self-interest, lust—can be used to control that person," she murmured at the window. "And often goes by the wayside if it gets in the way of other more important goals."

Her father again, most likely. "Only if the person using it against you doesn't understand love. Love is about wanting the best things for that person."

She slowly turned her head to blink at him. "That's a nice thought."

But she didn't believe it. Damn, her father had done a number on her. Will added her attitude about love to the list of hurdles he needed to navigate.

He reached for her hand resting on the console between them. "I would do anything, give anything, for my family. You're part of that now." He squeezed her hand for emphasis, then let her go and let that sink in.

Trying to bring things back to comfortable, Will pointed out various places as they drove into the main strip of the town. The grocery store was situated at the other end. Only being slightly over two miles wide and supporting a population of about two thousand, though that didn't count all the ranches in the area outside of town, still their destination gave him a chance to give her the full tour. He pointed out the feed store, and Pete's BBQ, the large animal vet clinic where Holly worked when she wasn't out on call, the bank, the dry cleaners, and so on. Most of the buildings were sided with age-blackened limestone, all two stories with awnings that stretched out over the sidewalks, everything landscaped with local trees and shrubs. They took pride in their town, which boasted several shops, a bar, and even a winery.

"I like this place," she said as he parked in the grocery store lot.

Will raised his eyebrows and pretended to consider the grocery store facade. "It's like any other grocery store."

She rolled her eyes. "No, the town, you goof."

"Yeah." He glanced outside, back down the main road. "It is nice."

They stepped out, smacking into a wall of humidity as the sun beat down on them. "Hot though," Rusty commented, fanning herself.

"August is worse," Will warned. Still, the blast of cool air when they walked through the double doors of the store was welcoming.

"Will Hill, you son of a gun."

Will cringed at the use of his name as well as at the voice, but turned with a polite smile. "Mike." He held out a hand to the man crossing the parking lot toward them.

Remembering his manners, he turned to Rusty, hand proprietorially at the small of her back. Hiding his reluctance, he introduced the two. "Rusty, this is Mike Jenkins. Mike, Rusty Walker—"

"So nice to meet you, ma'am." Mike thrust out a hand, interrupting Will's intro before he got to the most interesting part.

Will ignored the glance Rusty flicked his way as she shook Mike's hand. "Nice to meet you," she murmured.

Mike held on a tad too long, his gaze roving down Rusty's figure in jeans and a hot pink tank top. Will had to hide a smile at the snap of irritation in her eyes.

"Newcomers are always welcome," Mike said.

Somehow the guy managed to make it sound smarmy rather than kind.

Rusty's only response was a cursory smile that could've passed for a grimace. "Thanks," she said. "You didn't catch my full name, I'm afraid. It's Rusty Walker *Hill*."

Even through his shock that Rusty was the one to toss

that out there, Will almost laughed as the other man's shoulders sagged.

"Damn." Mike gave Will what he guessed was supposed to be a good-natured glare. "Should've known you Hills would snap up the newest eligible female in town," Mike grumbled.

Rusty lifted her eyebrows at Will in question.

"Cash married Holly who just moved back," he explained.

"I see." She turned to Mike. "We married before I got to town if that's any consolation."

"Not really." He grinned. "But congrats. And welcome to the area. I'm sure I'll see y'all around." With a tip of his hat, Mike sauntered off.

As they made their way to the stack of carts, Rusty eyed Will speculatively. "He's… friendly."

Only if he wanted something from someone. "Yeah. We were in the same class in school."

"I see," she murmured.

Did she? He suspected she might. Rusty didn't tend to get her head turned by a charming smile and good looks. Which was good news for Will. Charm was not one of his gifts.

"Were you competitive with each other?" she asked.

Will pulled a cart out of the neatly stacked line. "Mike could compete with a wall."

"Uh-huh. And you weren't at all." Skepticism lined the

words.

Will opened his eyes wide. "I have no idea what you're talking about."

She chuckled, brown eyes warm. "I bet." They paused in produce and she picked up a zucchini. Will blinked at the visual that provided, her handling the long vegetable put him in mind of those hands wrapped around part of his anatomy that strained to make that mental picture a reality.

He gave his head a shake. *Get your mind out of the gutter.*

"Do you not like being called Will Hill?" Her question pulled him back to the topic.

"Not really. Why do you ask?"

"Because you grimaced when he said it."

"Oh." Will grabbed a bunch of green bananas and tossed them in the cart. "No. Will Hill sounds like a Dr. Seuss character. Williams Hill sounds better."

"But you go by Will."

"Yeah." He blew out a breath with a shrug.

"So, what's the record?" she asked next.

He crossed his arms as he realized the question, but still played dumb. "What do you mean?"

She stopped at the tomatoes. "You know. The record you set that you were both going for."

His wife was a perceptive woman. He'd have to keep that in mind. "I still hold the school record for the mile in track."

"Figures. And what position did you play on the football team?"

Texas was football, and Will had been an athletic kid. But how'd she guess? "Wide receiver. Mike was quarterback."

"Ouch." She pursed her lips.

"I was voted team captain though." Now he was showing off like a teenager.

Jeez, he needed to get a grip.

That set her off laughing, drawing the attention of the few folks in there on Tuesday afternoon. "Of course, you were," she said through her giggles.

Next, she stopped at the cherries, and Will had to walk away before his mind and body embarrassed him. What was wrong with him anyway? The woman was shopping for fruits and vegetables, not here to do a strip tease just for him.

He needed space. So, he left the cart with a startled Rusty and went to get his own produce. By the time he returned, she was done with produce and they moved on to the aisles. He managed to keep his mind away from suggestive images the rest of the time in the store. Who knew produce could be so inadvertently evocative?

What he really needed was to give Rusty some space to get settled, and for his libido to calm the hell down. Maybe once they got into the groove of their respective roles, he could take it up a notch. But if he made a move now, she'd run.

She reminded him of a skittish filly—low on trust, ready to either lash out or run when she felt threatened.

Old-fashioned hard work and a routine, common goals were what he'd stick to for now. No matter how he excused it as a business deal to start, this wasn't just business, this was personal on a level that scared him. Because now that he had her, he didn't want to let her go.

He'd show her how life could be if she stayed, then he'd show her how *they* could be if she stayed.

Chapter Nine

Rusty picked at the roast on her plate as she did her best to present a happily newly married façade to Will's family gathered around the dinner table. The food was delicious, but she had bigger things on her mind. Like the bed in their room. One they'd shortly be sharing.

The rest of the day, Will had kept his touching and romance for when they had an audience. Otherwise, he treated her like one of the guys. Part of her relaxed at that, knowing he wasn't getting ideas from their situation. The other contrary half of her was getting her own ideas, and arguing with the logical side about how casual she and Will should keep things.

The man stirred feelings inside her no other man had set off before. When he touched her, she warmed up, wanting to lean into him. And, every so often, she'd catch a look in his eyes that would remind her of the kisses they'd shared. Not the ones for show, but the ones in her room.

How were they going to make it months sharing a room and not end up making use of that room for more than sleeping?

"Aren't you hungry, sweetie?" Evaline interrupted Rusty's thoughts.

Rats. She'd been caught fantasizing about the woman's son.

She glanced up to find all the Hills watching her. She sent them what she hoped was a convincing smile. "I'm never all that hungry after a long trip, but this roast is fantastic."

Did the excuse sound as flimsy to them as it did to her?

"Holly's the same way," Evaline said.

Apparently not.

"Maybe it's a girl thing, Mom," Jennings piped up. "Carter never did get into anything that required a lot of travel, but all of us boys did rodeo."

"Some still do," Will said.

"Yeah. Like me," Autry agreed.

Will lifted a single eyebrow. "When's the last rodeo you did?"

"The La Colina Sheriff's Posse this summer," Autry tossed back.

Jennings paused in serving up more mashed potatoes and snorted. "The only thing I saw you doing was Tara Hammond under the bleachers."

"Jennings Hill," Evaline gasped.

"What?" Jennings said around a bite. "I wasn't the one doing Tara Hammond under the bleachers."

"I wasn't doing her," Autry mumbled. "We were only

making out, Mom. I swear."

Rusty had to bite back a smile as the twenty-six-year-old grown cowboy tried to explain his sex life to his mother in an acceptable manner.

"I don't want to hear about you doing anything under the bleachers with a woman, even if it's just making out," Evaline said, her tone sharper than Rusty'd heard all day. Even Rusty would cower under her sharp eye.

"Yes, Mama," Autry murmured. He turned a bit red.

John Hill didn't say a word, but his stern presence at the head of the table as he watched the interaction between mother and son clearly said he'd back up his wife if asked.

Rusty waited for him to come down hard on Autry, but he said nothing. And, after a moment, all of them went back to eating and talking like nothing out of the ordinary had just happened.

Everyone except Rusty. That was it? Maybe the Hills yelled at each other behind closed doors?

Under the cover of the chatter, Will leaned over to murmur in her ear. "You look confused."

Was she that transparent? Damn. She'd have to work on her poker face. "Let's just say that scene would've gone down very differently at my house," she whispered back.

"Yeah?" he asked, obviously curious.

"Yeah. Dad was a lot of bark to go along with his bite." Garrett Walker had never laid a hand on her though.

She supposed she could be thankful for that. But he'd

tried to break her in other ways. Verbal ways.

Will considered her as though he could read between the lines and knew exactly how it had been for her. His gaze took in her upturned face for a long space of time while she held her breath. If she leaned forward slightly, maybe he'd...

Will dropped a casual kiss on her lips, and she gave a soft gasp even though she knew the kiss was for show. However, it mirrored her silent need so much, she couldn't help it.

He smiled. "Now you're with the Hills. We're not yellers."

Rusty's lips parted. So, he *had* read between the lines with ease. She wasn't quite sure how she felt about that.

"Hey, food hog, leave some for the rest of us," Autry snapped at Jennings, making Rusty jump at the sudden sound.

Will rolled his eyes. "Most of the time we're not yellers."

Dinner went smoothly after that. If she could count the casual snuggles Will gave her from time to time which amped up her heart rate. She helped clear the table, then insisted on helping with the dishes. Evaline refused to just let Rusty do it, but after some persuasion, at least allowed her to load the dishwasher.

Will, who had followed his dad and brothers out to the family room, eventually wandered back in. "There you are," he said.

Conscious Evaline was listening in and watching, and also aware Will had been doing most of the work to hold up their newlywed story, Rusty tossed him an amused smile. "Miss me?" she teased.

He grinned and took her up on the playful banter. Will stepped right in behind her, reaching around to pluck a dish out of the sudsy water even as he nuzzled her neck. "Yes, ma'am. I did."

He pressed into her, and to her shock, Rusty could feel exactly how much he'd missed her. She stiffened to keep herself from melting back against him like she really wanted to do. Will desired her, at least physically. Again, the specter of that bed loomed in her mind.

Months together in that room. Alone. What would be the harm in enjoying that time? Except it complicated the hell out of things—especially if they remained business partners after she left.

A hard kick of denial punched through her. She'd been married all of two and a half days and at the Hills less than twelve hours. Rusty stuffed the odd feeling she didn't want to leave down deep. She would be leaving when this was all over. She'd have a ranch to run.

Still, when he ran his lips down the sensitive skin at the side of her neck, she couldn't hold back her shiver.

"Would you two like some privacy?" Evaline interrupted the moment.

Despite the quiet amusement in the other woman's voice, Rusty still jumped. She was doing that a lot lately.

I really need to calm the hell down.

She dug an elbow into Will's ribs. He grunted, then retaliated by goosing her. Rusty squealed and jumped to the side. Then she spun to face his mother. "No need. I'm almost done. Then I think I'm going to bed early."

How could they forget they had an audience?

"You did have a long day," Evaline murmured. Still she couldn't hide her smile as she glanced between them.

She'd been taken in by their silly moment. Hell, so had Rusty. She turned back to the sink, a cloud of suspicion floating over her. Perhaps Will hadn't forgotten their audience and that had all been for show. Still, how could he fake his reaction to her?

She finished up the dishes as Will stood there silently watching. At least Evaline wasn't paying attention, busy with cleaning up. Still, his staring made her clumsy and she dropped the silverware more than once.

"Careful, there, butterfingers," he murmured after the third time.

"Why don't you go away?" she muttered out of the side of her mouth.

"And miss this chance to be with my new bride?" came the whispered reply.

So, it was about the appearance. She supposed that they'd have to keep the PDA dialed to high for a while, then they could turn down the volume of the lovey-dovey stuff.

"Hey, Will, I need some advice..." Jennings's voice floated down the hall before he appeared at the door.

Drying her hands on a dish towel, she took advantage of Will's distraction. "I'm beat. I'm going to bed." She went up on tiptoe and gave him a short kiss, though she was tempted to linger. "Night."

She'd made it all the way to the door when he spoke. "I won't be far behind you."

What did that mean? Did she have minutes or hours to try to be asleep when he came in? Because being awake was not an option. She'd been too tempted to take advantage. She smiled over her shoulder like that would be fine, then, as soon as she was out of view, rushed to the room.

She pulled PJs out of the drawer where she'd put them. Will had cleared out half his drawers for her, and given her half his closet. That had been plenty of space for her, though she suspected he was feeling a bit cramped. She'd already added a new set of drawers to her list of items to buy sooner rather than later. She didn't need anything fancy or large.

Dressed for bed, teeth and hair brushed, she stared at the bed. She should ask which side Will preferred, but she didn't want to go out to do so. Not dressed in hot pink shorts and a tight tank top to match. Common sense came to her rescue as she noticed one of the bedside tables already held Will's alarm clock and a book.

Fine. She'd take the other side.

Unfortunately, the other side meant getting on her hands and knees to try to get to the outlet for her alarm clock and her phone charger. She didn't hear the door open.

"There's a sight I never quite imagined when I thought of the first night home with my new bride." Dark laughter lurked in Will's voice.

She paused and crossed her eyes in annoyance. "Laugh it up, fuzzball."

To give him credit, she didn't hear any laughter. "You're quoting *Star Wars* at me now?"

Rusty didn't comment and continued messing with the plug. The soft click of the door, told her he'd closed it. "I'll be just a minute." She grunted as she struggled. "Your plug is a bit tough to reach."

"Take your time. I don't mind the view."

Rusty snorted at that. "We don't have an audience, Mr. Hill. So you can quit with the cutesy comments."

Silence greeted her comment, and she briefly wished she could see his face for his reaction. She hadn't meant to be quite so snippy with him.

"Do you need your big, strong husband to help?" Now his voice was coming from the other side of the bed. He'd obviously decided she was taking too long.

"No. I've got—" She extended her middle finger and managed to slot the charger into the plug. "Got it," she finished.

With a sigh, she backed out from under the bed to find Will at the drawers pulling out flannel PJ bottoms.

"Won't those be too hot?" she asked.

"I usually sleep in the raw." He glanced over his shoulder, eyebrows raised.

Oh. "Do you go commando too?" Rusty closed her eyes the second the words finished pouring from her mouth. Where the hell had her filters gone? Seemed as though she was in for a world of firsts for a while.

"No. I'm a boxers guy."

She snapped her eyes open and brazened it out. "I'd be fine if you slept in your boxers." No need for him to be miserable just because they had to maintain a semblance of propriety in this uber-strange situation.

"Thanks. That would be better." He turned to face her and stilled, his gaze trailing down her from head to toe in a sweep she felt in every single nerve ending as though he'd physically touched her. For the first time since they'd said *I do*, he appeared to be uncomfortable. "Do you need the bathroom?" he asked.

Not what she'd been expecting.

Rusty shook her head. "I already brushed my teeth and… stuff." She canted her head at the door. "It's all yours."

"Thanks."

They were starting to sound like awkward teenagers on a weird first date. Will disappeared into the bathroom, and Rusty took the opportunity to hop into bed. Only she was wide awake. No way could she lay here and pretend to be asleep by the time he came out.

"Shoot," she muttered. Then tossed back the covers.

If she was going to be awake, she needed something to occupy her mind. She dug around in her backpack and came up with her e-reader. Reading a book would relax her and be a signal that she wasn't interested in talking. Win-win. She also grabbed her glasses case.

A few minutes after she'd got settled, but was far from into the book—the words swimming on the page in front of her—Will finally emerged.

She glanced up. "I took the left side because it looks like you're already settled on the right side." She waved a hand at his bedside table. "I hope that's okay."

"That's fine."

Now he was the one giving off vibes that said he didn't want to get into a discussion. Fine with her. Rusty went back to her book, only his T-shirt suddenly registered and she laughed.

"What?" he asked.

"Your T-shirt looks familiar." She tipped her chin at his chest.

Will glanced down then chuckled. "I guess it does."

He was wearing the manly version of the one she'd had on the other day about adulting. Another gift from his family, no doubt.

She smiled. "When is your birthday by the way? As your wife, I should probably know these things."

"November second. Yours?"

"March third."

Will pulled back his side of the covers, then paused. "Would you prefer I sleep on top of the sheets, or maybe we put a pillow between us or something?"

Yes. Absolutely, yes. But she didn't say so, because no way would she give him any hint this bothered her. "No. That's okay. We're both adults."

Besides, a pillow or a sheet would be a token barrier if they really wanted to…

Rusty gave herself a mental shake. *You don't want to.*

WHAT WILL WANTED to do, which was pull her up against his body, was way out of the question. Hell, they needed to get past kissing having the effect of sending her hot-foot in the other direction before they took it to that level. The pillow suggestion was more for him than for her, not that it would be much of a deterrent. Still, something was better than nothing.

He slipped between the sheets and pretended not to notice when his weight had her sliding toward him, or the way she scooted to the very edge of the bed to overcorrect. Taking a leaf from her example, he picked up the book he'd been reading for a while. But after he'd read the same page three times without absorbing a single word, he gave up and put it down.

Instead, he turned on his side to face Rusty.

He'd meant to give her more time to get settled before joining her in the room. But he'd helped Autry with a decision about selling some stock, then he'd sat in the family room with his parents and brothers, making small talk, and watching the minute hand on the old-fashioned clock on the mantel tick off each agonizing minute. Fifteen was about as much as he'd handled before jumping up, receiving twin grins of devilry from Autry and Jennings.

Jennings passed Autry a five-dollar bill, and Will had raised his eyebrows.

Jennings shrugged. "We had a bet going as to how long you'd hold out before joining your new wife. I said ten minutes, Autry said fifteen."

He'd ignored his brothers' shenanigans and said a general good night to the room before heading down the hall to his bedroom. Perhaps the time had come to build his own place on the ranch, separate from the main house.

He had no idea what he'd expected when he came into the room. It certainly hadn't been a view of Rusty's nicely rounded backside in short shorts as she squished under his bed. Will hadn't known if he should laugh, offer to help, or groan as her position put him in mind of what he'd like to do to her, and with her, and... Hell.

He'd gone with the first two options, not that she'd accepted the help.

After a minute, Rusty flicked him a sideways glance. "You're staring," she said.

"Yup."

Her lips clamped tightly and Will held in a chuckle, but didn't stop. Why not stare? Rusty was one of the most beautiful things he'd ever seen. Surprisingly dark lashes brushed her cheeks when she blinked. Her full lips, even tight with annoyance, were fantasy inducing. And he had the almost uncontrollable urge to wrap a lock of her fiery hair around his finger and savor the silky texture.

Her breasts, outlined by the soft material of her tank top, rose and fell with a huff. "Do you need something?" she demanded.

"Can't a man look at his wife?" he asked.

She eyed him over the rim of her glasses. Another thing he hadn't expected—the purple rimmed reading glasses gave her a studious air that he found... damn adorable.

"Not his fake wife," she said.

Then she returned her attention to her book. Will stopped resisting, reaching for a curl that lay against her arm. Usually she kept it back in a braid. He liked it down.

Rusty tensed at the move. "What are you doing?" she asked after a moment.

"Seeing how soft your hair is." Seemed pretty obvious to him.

"Why?"

Will shrugged. "Doing this, instead of what I really want to do, seemed like a good idea."

The tip of her pink tongue snaked out to wet her lips.

After a moment, she put her e-reader down and turned her head to face him.

"I find that very distracting. Do you mind?"

Will chuckled but released her and rolled to his back. "My apologies, ma'am, I'm just not used to having someone in here with me. I find *you* distracting."

Rather than resume reading, she canted her head in his direction. "No way do I believe you've never had a woman in your bed."

He hitched his mouth up. "Why, Mrs. Hill, are you saying you find me attractive?"

She snorted. "You know you are. Stop fishing."

That was the first he'd heard of it, as generic as her answer was. His poor ego soaked in the small give on her part. "To answer your question, I've never taken a woman to this room, out of respect for my parents."

"Oh." She sat quietly for a beat. Then a giggle suddenly escaped her, the sound going straight to his already hard crotch.

"What?" Will asked.

"I'm picturing Dad's reaction if I'd ever taken a guy to my room at home."

"Given your tendency to push his buttons, I'm surprised you didn't do something like that on purpose."

She rolled her eyes expressively. "I had zero wish to be party to murder."

Someone banged on Will's door with a fist and Rusty

jumped.

"Better not hear anything inappropriate from you two," Autry called through the door.

"Go away," Will called back. "We're busy."

Rusty smacked his arm as Autry's laughter faded down the hallway, but he just winked. "We have to keep up the appearance, honey."

"Are all brothers this annoying?" she asked, her brows drawn into a frown.

A tug in the region of his heart had Will turning to her, a hand on her leg through the blanket, because she'd lost her own brother before they'd had a grown relationship. "Autry is harmless."

"Oh, I know." She waved away the comment. "I don't mind."

"In fact, he might be a tad jealous."

"What?" She snorted inelegantly. And even that was cute. "No way."

"Sweetheart, you seem to have no idea how beautiful you are. Autry is usually the Hill with all the prettiest women. Having me snag the prize before him is a bit of a switch up."

"That surprises me," she said. Then glanced away, as though she hadn't meant to voice that out loud.

A fact which caught his full attention. "Which part?"

Her lips pursed. "The part about Autry being the Hill with the prettiest woman. No offence to your brother, but I bet many of those women would've gone for you if you crooked a finger."

Will grinned. "Are you saying, in a roundabout way, that you find me more attractive than my brothers?"

She shifted, sort of twitching her shoulders. "Well... I haven't got to know them yet."

So, yes. Warmth lit in the region of his heart. "I'm glad."

That drew her gaze, and something in her eyes seemed to soften. "What do you really want to do?"

Her eyes widened. Again, he got the impression she'd spoken without thinking. And had her voice gone all husky?

"What do I want to do?" he asked.

She nodded slowly, not looking away. "You said that you were playing with my hair instead of doing what you wanted. What do you want?"

The air punched from his lungs. Did she mean what he thought? "If I tell you, you'll run a mile." Or slap his face.

Holy hell, he shouldn't be rushing this. Where had his control gone? Apparently close proximity to this woman knocked it clear out of his head.

"Try me," Rusty said.

He considered her for a long moment—soft breasts rising and falling quickly, a pink hue in her cheeks, but deep brown eyes steady. Did she really want to know? His tightened, like a vice had wrapped around his ribs while every other part of him hardened to painful levels.

"I'd rather show you."

Slowly, giving her every opportunity to pull away or stop

him, Will moved his hand and brushed up her arm, over her delicate collarbone, then traced the dipping neckline of her top. Her breathing hitched at his touch, but she didn't stop him.

His own breathing sounded too loud in his ears. "I should stop."

Only he didn't. Instead, he hooked a finger in her top and pulled it down, exposing a ripe, rose-colored nipple already standing to attention, begging for his touch.

"Why?" she asked, voice ragged now.

"You need time to adjust to all this." He tweaked her nipple and a tiny whimper escaped her. "You have to be reeling from all the changes in your life."

"Sounds sensible," she whispered.

A glance at her face showed her watching his hands, her eyes glittering, her expression tight, reflecting his own need. He rolled her nipple between his fingers, relishing the shiver that made her tremble.

At the same time, though, a voice of responsibility niggled at the back of his mind. Will pulled his hand away. Closing his eyes, he swallowed, reaching for a control he wasn't sure he'd find.

"Don't stop," Rusty begged.

He opened his eyes to find hers closed as well. "I don't want to take advantage of you," he said.

Her long lashes fluttered up so she could look at him.

A headache started behind his eyes, probably from how

hard he was clenching his jaw to keep his hands off. "I owe you the knowledge that you are safe here with me," he insisted.

Will flopped back against his pillow and flung an arm over his eyes. Lord, what had he been thinking? That was just it, though. *He* wasn't thinking, his dick was.

"You're right," she said, so quietly he almost didn't catch it.

The bed rustled as Rusty moved around. After a second she stopped and he glanced over, from beneath his arm to find she'd rearranged her clothes. Then she scooted down under the covers and turned off her bedside lamp. He did the same, and kept his back firmly to her as he lay down.

"You're a good man, Williams Hill."

Her voice drifted to him in the darkness, and Will swallowed again. He was trying dammit, but sometimes being good sucked.

Chapter Ten

"DAMN THAT WOMAN can sit a horse."

"Yeah. I could watch her all day long."

Will paused in unloading bales of hay from his truck into the barn as the conversation going on between Jordan and Chris caught his attention.

He fought back a spurt of irritation. Men admired women in general, and cowboys admired a woman who could sit a horse. They weren't saying anything inappropriate, necessarily. He had no reason to want to bust their heads together and send them off with their tails tucked between their legs.

He should leave it alone and get on with his work. Still, he made his way down the length of the barn to where the back side opened into a covered arena where Rusty preferred to work her horses most often. Chris and Jordan were perched on the metal fence ringing the soft dirt of the large space, watching as she took one of her horses through various exercises designed to train it to turn around a barrel quickly.

This was a greener horse, and a bit nervous. He kept hopping away from the barrel, out from under her, and she held her seat every time. She also had infinite patience and gentle hands on the reins. He had zero doubts she'd know the best way to calm the jumpy animal and work those fears out of him.

And Chris and Jordan were right. Rusty was a thing of beauty to watch—the deep red hair hanging down her back in a long ponytail, the toned curve of her body on display in jeans and a black T-shirt—this one read "Girlz Rule" in pink glitter—and perfectly in control of the large animal between her thighs.

Dammit. A few weeks into her stint at High Hill Ranch and thoughts like those only plagued him more frequently. Lying beside her night after night, her rose-sweet scent imbedded into his pillow, didn't help matters any.

He crossed his arms. "Don't you two have some horses to be prepping for Rusty?"

Jordan and Chris jumped at the sound of his voice. They exchanged a glance and hopped off the fence.

"Yes, boss," Chris mumbled. Each tipped his hat as he hustled past Will and into the barn.

Hell. Now he was snapping at his hands and acting all proprietorial about his wife. Even his mother had commented about his touchy mood lately.

"Hey." Rusty rode up to where he stood beside the opening into the arena. "What do you think?" she asked.

Obviously, she was asking about her work with the horse. "He's coming along," Will said.

"Yeah." She frowned.

"Problem?" he asked.

Rusty narrowed her eyes at the question. "Yes, Will. What do you *think*?"

"You need to break his hind quarters loose. He's pulling with the front, more than pushing with the back. He's losing forward motion when he's curving around your foot."

Rusty was already nodding. "Got it. Thanks."

Without another word, she turned the horse back into the arena, and started another exercise, one that involved keeping the horse's nose down and faced where he was going. At the same time, she'd heel into one side, curving the horse around her leg and forcing his hind quarters to be doing the work. Then she'd let him out of it.

The horse kept throwing his head up, or losing forward momentum. Will knew the exercise. Rusty would do that over and over for days until the horse would do it naturally without tossing his head or losing the forward movement.

She was in it, so Will turned and left her to it. He needed to get the hay unloaded anyway, no matter how much he wanted to stay and enjoy the view.

On his way past the boys, he gave both a friendly nod. No need to run the tyrant over these fellas for no good reason. They knew what they were doing. Hell, they were friends. They shouldn't suffer because he was hard every minute of the day and getting no relief. Cold showers and hand jobs weren't helping enough. If anything, they added to his irritation levels.

And that was just the physical side. Gaining Rusty's trust in this relationship was proving an exercise in patience.

By six o'clock, Will made his way to his office in the barn. He and Rusty talked at the end of every day about her progress, changes that needed to be made, and next steps for upcoming clients or searching out new ones.

She was still brushing out a white mare she'd recently started working with. At the same time, she was on her cell phone, though he couldn't tell who with. A quick nod told him she'd meet him when she was done, so Will sat down behind his desk and got started on some paperwork he'd been avoiding.

"Phew," she said as she breezed in, closing the door behind her. His office was the only air-conditioned part of the barn.

Rusty dropped into a chair, fanning herself. "It was a scorcher today," she said.

Even drenched in sweat, and covered in a fine layer of dust, and smelling of horse and leather, she was still gorgeous. "Hotter tomorrow," he said. "I'd skip a day if I were you. It'll be too hot for the horses to be out there working, even in the shaded arena."

She nodded as she wiped her sleeve across her forehead. "You're the boss, boss."

Yes. I am.

Not exactly a happy thought these days. At least not in relation to one Rusty Hill. Because progress in the area of his wife had been zilch.

"Was that your dad on the phone?" he asked.

Her lips went flat. "No. That was Doris. He was out somewhere she couldn't reach."

"How's he doing?"

"She says pretty well. No major physical signs yet."

"That's great!" Rusty's relationship with her father was complicated, but Will had a sneaking suspicion she still cared about the old man.

"He told her to ask if we're pregnant yet." Rusty just shook her head.

Huh. "I guess he wants to hold on to see his first grandchild."

Rusty snorted. "He's not that sentimental." She sighed. "Do you mind if we drop this?"

And there she went, shutting down, shutting him out again. "Sure. Give me a sec to wrap this up, then we can talk horses."

"What are you working on?" she asked.

"Projections for end of year revenue." He glanced back at the computer. "In fact, while I've got you. You should finish up with three of the horses, and we already have an offer for that bay mare you're done with. So that should add up to…"

He paused to check his figures.

"Eighty-six thousand. Assuming they come here to get them. If you add in shipping costs plus taxes, then…" She glanced up at the ceiling as she calculated more then rattled off a figure down to the dollar.

Smart and beautiful. "I think I married up," Will said.

She just rolled her eyes.

Recognizing he'd made her uncomfortable, Will let it go. Instead he grabbed a water bottle from the small fridge he kept in his office and tossed it to her. "Give me the rundown."

After a few long swallows, Rusty launched in to her usual daily report. Will loved this part of the day. Talking horses and business with a woman who got him like people rarely did was always stimulating. He loved the way her mind worked, so similar to his thinking when it came to the best way to train horses. In fact, he loved it best when they debated the best technique to try next. Between the two of them, they were an encyclopedia of horse knowledge.

Granted, he often had to send her off to shower before dinner without him. He couldn't stand up from behind his desk, because the damn woman was stimulating more than his mind. Still, the best hour of his day was this one right here.

He glanced at the clock as she started winding down, touching on the horses she hadn't worked today but would in two days after the heat wave dropped. Damn, that'd gone fast.

Too fast.

He didn't want to let her walk away.

"Has anyone mentioned the swimming hole to you, yet?"

he asked.

Rusty blinked as the question interrupted her mid-sentence. "Um… No."

"It's a natural cold spring, three actually, which feed Little Big Creek that runs through our property on the southern side. Great place to cool off in the evenings after heat like today. What do you say?"

Big brown eyes stared at him like he'd lost his ever-loving mind for a long minute. "You're asking me to go swimming with you?"

He thought he'd been pretty clear. Will pushed the brim of his hat up so she could see his face better. "Yes'm. That's what I'm asking."

"Tonight?"

Now he smiled. "If you're busy, I guess tomorrow would work too. But you look hot and tired right now, so I figured cooling off that way would appeal."

"What about dinner?" she asked next.

"How about I pack us up something to take along? Mom won't mind. In fact, she'd love it."

Her eyebrows, which had been reaching for her hairline, settled back into their normal position. "Oh, your family goes on hot nights. Yeah, I'd love to come."

"It'll just be us," he was compelled to end that misunderstanding.

"Oh." She blinked at him again. "Why?"

Will laughed as he stood up from behind his desk. His

laugher was as much for him as for her, because hell if he knew how to convince his wife that he was interested in her. "I thought you might enjoy it. Besides, it'll help with our newlyweds story."

"Mmmm…" she hummed. "Autry and Jennings were teasing me the other day about how I'm a low-maintenance wife."

Will frowned, but she held up her hands. "Don't worry. They were just joking."

Maybe. But obviously he needed to step it up in front of his family. A few dates would help.

Hand at her back, he gave her a little shove out of his office. "You go get a bathing suit on under your gear. Bring a towel and a change of clothes. I'll grab my own after I get the food and have the horses ready to go. Meet back here."

"All right." She finally acquiesced, though the way he was hustling her out of the barn didn't give her much time to protest.

She walked off in the direction of the bunkhouse, and Will stood for a minute watching the gentle sway of her hips as she went. *Jeez, I'm a glutton for self-inflicted punishment.*

RUSTY HELD UP two bathing suits, wasting precious time debating which to go with. She didn't own a one-piece thanks to her juvenile need to drive her father nuts. So, the question was did she go with the neon eighties-style suit that had a more modest bandeaux top but showed some thigh, or did she go with the black suit which was more conservative on the bottom, but barely covered her breasts?

I should tell Will I don't want to go.

The trouble was, she did want to go. Swimming in a cool spring sounded wonderful after her hot, sweaty, grimy day. And, if she was honest with herself, spending some time with Will without the entire family watching their every move or in their room pretending to fall asleep was also appealing.

Rusty scowled.

Spending any time with Will had gotten more and more appealing with every passing day. She'd been able to work with horses all day long without interruption or interference. She discussed her work every evening with Will. He listened, he gave opinions that she respected, not only because they were well thought out but because he couched them in a way that never demanded or insisted. They were opinions or suggestions, and that was all.

He trusted her to do her job.

She'd never had that at home. Granted, she found herself caught up watching him. His blue eyes lit up when he talked about horses. Will truly loved what he did for a living, and his passion was contagious. The hour they spent together talking at the end of the day was quickly becoming her favorite time of every day.

And that was not good.

Even though she loved how his mind worked, how they connected through their love of horses, her brain still recognized the need to keep her distance. When she inherited Rising Star, she would move back up to Wyoming, and this relationship would be all business. Why risk the pain of a breakup when this was only temporary? Too bad her body wasn't on the same wavelength. She woke most every night throbbing with need. She'd had to take care of herself in the shower almost every morning and some evenings. She'd never experienced anything like it.

But that didn't matter. Why would she screw up such a good situation with messy stuff like hormones and lust? Will had obviously drawn a professional line between them after that first night, only touching her when his family was around, and otherwise treating her more or less like an employee. She was determined to keep it the same.

"Guess it'll have to be the neon suit," she muttered.

Quickly she pulled the suit on, then dressed in her already nasty jeans and shirt since she'd just be getting on another horse. In a bag, she stuffed a towel and a change of clothes. Then, trying not to be too eager about it, she headed back to the barn.

Evaline caught her in the kitchen. "You look eager." Her mother-in-law smiled.

"The swimming hole sounds wonderful after being in the heat all day." Rusty tried to downplay the fact she'd been practically skipping out the door.

"I'll bet. Of course, some alone time with Will probably appeals too."

"We don't get much alone time," Rusty murmured.

Had this been her father, Rusty would've worried that a double meaning applied to the comment, that Evaline was concerned or suspicious about their relationship. But she could tell by the open, honest expression on Evaline's face that wasn't the case. Will's mother truly was a sweetheart, always including Rusty in the conversation or asking about her own experiences or shooing Jennings and Autry away when they appeared to be pestering her.

"Part of living on a family ranch." Evaline nodded in understanding. "Will was just saying you two needed a date night."

He was? When was that? "That would be… nice."

"You better get going." She was shooed away. "Will's already out there."

She found Will in the barn, strapping a few packs to their horses' saddles. The food, she assumed. He grinned when he saw her, and Rusty couldn't stop an answering grin.

"Ready?" he asked.

"To cool off in a spring-fed swimming hole? Absolutely." *That's right, girl. Keep it about enjoying the activity.* Nothing to do with the man.

"All right." He laced his fingers to give her a leg up.

He'd picked Lady Luck for her—a lovely bay mare who loved to run fast. Then he mounted his own horse. Shadow was a big black brute who was actually a softy underneath that intimidating size. Both horses pranced, seemingly eager to get a move on as well.

The ride wasn't a particularly long one, taking them around a half hour, though they did give their horses their heads for a while. Rusty laughed, exhilarated as her mount flew over the undulating ground and Will beside her. She pulled up when he did, setting their horses to a walk. Eventually, he led her down an embankment to a small river which pooled at a natural bend in the land.

"You really love to ride," he commented as they dismounted.

"So do you." She undid the packs from the saddle, then started loosening Lady Luck's girth. The sweet horse had earned a nice laze in the shade.

"True." He patted Shadow's neck. "Did you leave your own horse at Rising Star?"

Rusty stiffened a bit, she couldn't help it.

Will frowned over Shadow's back at her. "You don't have to tell me if I'm being a nosy jerk."

She shook her head. "It's okay. Most of the horses I had at the ranch were ones I trained for other people. My horse, Sadie, died last year."

"I'm sorry."

She scrunched up her nose against the sting in her eyes. "Thanks. She was six when Dad bought her for me. I was only six myself at the time. She lived a long, happy life."

"You didn't buy a new horse?"

"Nah." She twitched a shoulder in an attempted shrug, but he must've caught that it wasn't as casual as she'd like to play off.

"Why not?" he pressed.

"By then I'd finished college and had come home. I was determined to make my own way, rather than live off Daddy's charity." She rolled her eyes. "I lived off the money I made training horses, but helping with the rodeo stock limited how many I could take on at once. So money went to things like my truck and trailer, rather than a horse for me."

"I see."

They didn't talk for a few minutes as they unpacked the bags and laid out a picnic blanket and the food.

"Swim or eat first?" Will asked.

The cool water beckoned. "Definitely swim," she said.

Without thinking about it, she whipped her shirt over her head, dropping it on the blanket, then toed off her boots and zipped out of her jeans, which stuck a bit thanks to the heat and humidity and her sweat. Still she managed to get them off, then glanced up to find Will, his hands at the button of his jeans but not moving, his body still as he watched her.

Damn the man looked good without a shirt—his cowboy-lean body muscled in a way that made her want to do bad things. Dangerous things. Inappropriate things.

Don't screw up a good thing. Other than the constant state of arousal issue, they'd settled into an easy relationship.

"Come on, slow poke," she urged. "Get a move on."

She didn't wait for him and waded right into the water, the mud squishing between her toes gross, but worth dealing with as cool water enveloped her body. With a blissful sigh, she slipped beneath, letting the pond wash away the dirt and sweat of the day.

She came back up to find Will had joined her and obviously dunked under as well. His dark hair was wet and slicked back.

"You were right, this is fantastic." She gave a happy little sigh.

"It's one of my favorite places to come in the summer," he admitted.

"I can see why." She skimmed her hand over the surface, enjoying the sensations as the chilled water slid over her skin.

"So..." Will paused. "If you were so determined to be independent, why'd you go home after college?"

Ah. Back to the conversation they'd been having a minute ago. At least it would take her mind off the half-naked man standing not three feet from her, and how she wanted to close the distance. One would think she'd be used to resisting him after all the time sharing a bed.

She should've known his question would come anyway. What surprised her though, wasn't the question, but the fact that she wanted to tell him. Will was... easy to be with. And she trusted anything she told him would be kept in strict confidence.

She kept her gaze trained on the sky over the water—starkly blue and turning toward evening colors with hints of pinks and peaches. A few lazy white clouds floated along. "I assumed Rising Star would be mine one day, and was determined to learn the business."

"So, you tried to what… prove yourself to your father for years?"

She shrugged. "Something like that."

"That's bullshit," Will snapped.

Rusty bobbled in the water, eyes flying wide, mouth open.

"What?" Will asked.

"You swore," she squeaked.

He laughed. "I swear a lot, just not in the presence of a lady." He tipped an imaginary hat in her direction.

Rusty chuckled. "Still. You swore."

He shrugged. Was that… Was he blushing? No way. It had to be a reaction to the cold water.

"It's just that you are so obviously qualified to run that ranch. Your dad's attitude is ridiculous," he said by way of explanation.

For the second time in as many minutes, she stared at him with wide eyes.

In response, he slid closer to her in the water. "I mean it, Rusty."

"I can tell," she murmured, her voice a bit croaky.

He really did believe in her like that, she could tell by the intent look in his eyes. And the swearing.

A balloon of emotions she couldn't quite sort out expanded inside her chest. No one had believed in her like that since Reed. But could she trust it? Not just her father, but those love interests who'd turned out to only be in it for the connection to Garrett Walker and Rising Star Ranch had left her with a sour taste in her mouth when it came to men. Maybe Will was truly different... and maybe not.

Will took her by the shoulders, pulling her from her thoughts. "Your dad is an outdated ass if he doesn't see that." Serious blue eyes stared into hers, as though he was trying to make her see he was right.

Rusty closed her mouth before she accidentally swallowed a mosquito or something. Or kissed him, which would be way worse.

"Thanks. I think, way deep down—" She rolled her eyes again. "Dad knows that. This move with the inheritance is more about forcing me into something he wants for me."

He cocked his head. "Marriage."

"A guaranteed male heir he approves of."

His hands, still on her shoulders, tightened. "Excuse me?"

She puffed out a breath, not sure if his touch or finally admitting this out loud was messing with her equilibrium more. "A man by my side to make sure his legacy is handled the right way."

He stared at her silently for a long moment. "You believe that?"

She couldn't quite pinpoint the something in his voice. Almost like he was concerned and angry at the same time. "Yes. He's never loved anything more than Rising Star. Not even his children. Reed came close, I guess, and maybe my mother. At least according to Doris. When Mom died, Dad turned… bitter. But I won't let his bitterness ruin my life."

His hands relaxed a fraction on her shoulders. "Good for you."

Yeah. Only now she couldn't look away from his blue eyes. And she didn't want him to take his hands away. Rusty stared up at Will, her emotions a swirl of conflicting needs, and silently urged him to stay, to step closer, to…

He slid his hands down her arms, stepping in close enough she could feel his heat even through the chilly water.

He linked his fingers with hers, and slowly lowered his head. When his lips hovered above hers, barely out of reach, he stopped. "I'm going to kiss you now."

She huffed out a laugh. "Good for you." She parroted his words.

He chuckled even as he brushed his lips over hers. Once. Twice. Then his arms went around her, pulling her up close against his body, skin to skin. He swiped his tongue over the seam of her lips, demanding entrance, which she happily gave, opening for him.

Rusty lifted her arms, wrapping them around his neck. The water buoyed her weight, and she lifted her legs, to wrap them around his waist, giving her easier access to his mouth. At the same time, the hard bulge pressing against her told her the cold water was no deterrent for his interest.

She shuddered at the evidence of his arousal. He'd been so casual with her since that night in their room, she'd almost wondered if it had even happened, if his interest had been real. But this was real. His hard heat and his mouth on hers were real.

Maybe she could enjoy him… just for a little bit… just while she was here…

Sensations engulfed her, and her mind went hazy as she enjoyed every slide of this tongue, every nip of his lips, the way his hands spanned her waist, the feel of his muscled chest against her breasts.

He tasted like peppermint and she vaguely realized that, like her, he'd brushed his teeth before coming out together. Had he realized this would happen? Hoped for it? Because she definitely had, even if she didn't want to admit it to herself.

A rough hand ran up over her hip, the dip of her waist, brushing her ribs to cover a breast, and she shuddered, her nipple hardening.

"We should stop," Will murmured between kisses.

"Yeah," she murmured back.

But he didn't and neither did she.

Instead, he sucked her lower lip between his teeth and Rusty rubbed against the hot hard part of him, the pressure beautiful and right where she needed it.

Suddenly, Will hitched his hands under her ass and spun them in the water, then plowed toward the shore. Once on dry land, he laid her down on the blanket, coming down on top of her, between her legs. They were soaking the blanket, and the ground was hard and rocky under her back, but she was too far gone to care, because Will kept kissing her.

The tempo of his kisses changed, from desperate and fast to slow and thorough. Very thorough. Meanwhile his hands explored every inch of her skin. He flipped her bathing suit top aside, and tweaked her straining nipple, drawing a moan from her lips.

He grinned. "You like that?"

She could only nod.

In answer, he dipped his dark head to draw her nipple into the warm recess of his mouth, torturing her with tongue and teeth until she was a panting mass of sensation beneath him. She speared her hands through his wet hair, cool against her fingertips, to hold him there.

Eventually, he released her to raise his head and pin her with a glittering blue gaze. "I want you."

She grinned and deliberately shifted, rubbing against his hard length. "I hadn't guessed."

He chuckled and dropped his head to kiss her briefly, as though he couldn't stop himself. She reached out to try to bring him back, but he snagged her by the wrists and shook his head. "We have a... bit of a problem."

Rusty raised her eyebrows. "We shouldn't?"

He grimaced but shook his head. "That too, I guess. But no. Our problem is we have no condoms with us."

Rusty smacked headfirst into reality with a painful thump. She dropped back against the blanket as breath hissed between her teeth. "Damn."

The fever of desire hadn't left her, and she briefly debated offering up her oral services, but they'd both been working hard all day, and a dip in river water didn't exactly wash that kind of grime away.

She closed her eyes and groaned. "Damn," she said again.

WILL DROPPED HIS forehead to hers. "My thoughts exactly."

Being a responsible man had never sucked so much as it did right now. Rusty lay under him, almost naked, every glorious inch of her skin pressed against his, her lips swollen from his kisses, and, for once, not running a country mile form his touch. His body, meanwhile, remained painfully hard.

"I guess..." He took a deep breath. "I guess we should get dressed and eat."

"Yeah." At least Rusty didn't sound any happier about it than he did. That was... progress at least.

To keep the awkward to a minimum, Will averted his eyes as he rolled away from her, giving her a second to rearrange her bathing suit, covering breasts he'd just had his hands on, his mouth. He took a moment to collect himself as well, willing his hard-on to calm down. But his body was too keyed up.

"Um…" Rusty's voice came from further behind him. He glanced over to find her already dressed. "Do you mind if we skip the food and head back?"

"Sure. No problem." Food and casual chitchat weren't exactly high on his list of things to do right now either.

In short order, he dressed, they packed everything back up and headed back. A long, uncomfortable ride—both because of their silence and because of his dick—they made it to the barn. "I'll take care of the horses," he said.

She looked at him, maybe for the first time since they got on their horses, her brown eyes unfathomable. "Thanks."

Only he couldn't let her go like this. As she passed him, Will reached out to snag her by the wrist. He only meant to tug her back around to face him, meaning to ask if she was okay, or some vague notion along those line. Only she let out a little whimper of need that so matched his own churning need, he tugged her into him, and took her mouth in a long kiss, savoring the way her body melted into his.

Kissing Rusty could become addictive.

Eventually the kisses slowed, and he raised his head. She slowly opened her eyes, but he knew the look. Regret.

"We shouldn't," she whispered as she shook her head.

But she didn't step back, or take her arms from around his waist.

"Because I'm your fake husband?" he asked.

Her lips kicked up in a half-smile that appeared more sad than amused. Did she regret the fake part? Or the husband part?

"Yes," she said. "But eventually, this ends. Then all we are are business partners. I get the ranch, you get Rising Star as an exclusive partner. Win-win. Throwing more into this already complicated mess would be too much of a risk."

With a deep breath, she released him and stepped back. And he let her go, mostly because breathing had become painfully difficult. She might want him, but it looked as though she would never let herself see him as more.

He put his hands on his hips, staring at the ground as he wrestled for control. He wanted to argue with her, to insist the chemistry between them was bigger than a fling. But he couldn't guarantee it. And if it ended, working together as closely as they did would be too hard if they took it further and he couldn't convince her to stay.

"You're right," he finally agreed. Or was he being a damn coward?

She laughed, maybe at the reluctance in his voice, the frustration with the situation. Whatever... she didn't sound amused so much as resigned. "I know. Dammit."

Then, without another word, she spun on her bootheel and walked out of the barn. And he let her go.

Chapter Eleven

RUSTY SAT IN one of the rocking chairs on the front porch, a citronella candle on the small table beside her keeping the mosquitoes away, and stared into the endless stars. She had her knees drawn up and her arms wrapped around them. A rare cool breeze in early September, when the heat of the summer continued to linger, lifted strands of her hair off her neck.

She'd been driven out here after a call with her dad. After weeks of trying to talk to the man and only getting Doris because he was constantly out, she'd finally got him on the phone. He'd certainly sounded the same. But what had driven her out here was another question about babies.

"We just got married, Dad, and hardly knew each other when we did. Give us some time, okay?"

"No time like the present," he'd insisted.

That had only degraded into a stubborn standoff about the decisions she was making in her life. In less than five minutes he'd managed to call her an old maid and warn her she'd lose her husband if she didn't start producing.

Eventually, they'd both hung up angry before she could

talk about when she and Will would be out for their first visit. Now that things had settled here, as much as they could, she wanted to get home. Her father might be a controlling, closed-off ass, but he was still her father. And her remaining time with him was limited.

She'd call again tomorrow and get it arranged.

Her momentary escape to the porch didn't last too long. Headlights showed off in the distance for a while until a small white car pulled up in front of the house, rather than the back. A woman hopped out and grabbed a suitcase from the trunk before making her way up the stairs. As soon as the lights hit her face, Rusty knew exactly who she was.

"You must be Carter," she called.

Carter's dark hair, cut in a chic bob, swung against her cheeks as she sharply turned her head. Her frown cleared as her gaze landed on Rusty.

Then she grinned. "And you must be my new sister-in-law."

Not quite two months into their marriage, and Rusty was starting to get more comfortable with that title. Rather than the usual pang at lying that accompanied the reminder, a strange warmth settled in the region of her heart. A sensation she stuffed down deep because allowing herself to truly feel a part of this family was a bad idea.

Still, she returned the smile and hopped up to greet Carter properly. Her father, despite all his faults, had certainly taught her manners. To her surprise, Carter dropped her suitcase and pulled Rusty in for a hug.

"You must be a special woman to have captured Will's heart," Carter murmured before releasing her.

There was the pang of guilt, and the oddest wish she was *that* special. Hell, this fake marriage was messing with her mind.

"He is a great guy." She left it at that.

"Mind if I join you?" Carter waved at the rocking chairs.

"Sure." Rusty resumed her seat, and Carter dropped into the other chair beside her with a heavy sigh.

"Long drive?" Rusty asked.

"Yeah. Longer week. My boss is such a hardass."

"Is this at the law firm you're consulting for while you're getting your PhD?" Rusty asked.

Carter nodded. "Yeah. Jonas, the man who heads up the firm, is a workaholic and expects everyone else to follow his lead." She grimaced.

"Must be tough to have a boyfriend over an hour away when you've got a boss with those expectations," Rusty murmured.

Carter flicked her a surprised glance, then chuckled. "I'm so used to Austin where everyone minds their own business that I forget about small-town talk." She sighed. "Brian proposed."

Rusty's eyes flew wide. Why hadn't anyone in the family told her that? Unless it was new? And Carter didn't exactly seem elated.

"Ummm... Is this recent?" Rusty asked, trying to navigate the tricky conversation.

"Tonight, actually. I saw him first before coming home."

"Oh." Rusty gave herself a shake at that underrated response. "Congrats!"

"I told him I'd think about it."

"Oh." This time Rusty had no idea how to respond, so she said nothing.

She took in Carter's expression—a mixture of confusion and weariness, dark circles under her eyes and a small frown puckering her brows. The woman looked torn.

"I know it's none of my business, but I'm new to the family and I don't know you or Brian. Maybe it would help to talk it out?"

Carter blinked at her with the blue eyes the Hill family shared. "I can see why Will fell for you," she finally murmured.

Rusty had no idea why Carter would see that, but forced her lips into a smile as an expected response. "I'm good at keeping things confidential, but I don't think that's why."

Carter chuckled. "No. You're a horsewoman and gorgeous. I'm guessing those were the initial draws."

Rusty blinked, but kept her thoughts to herself, letting Carter sit and think.

For her part, Carter leaned her head against the chair, her gaze focused outward, on the star-filled sky maybe. "I love Brian. I do," she said. "He's a terrific guy—smart, funny, a great kisser." A soft smile played around her mouth.

"But?" Rusty asked.

Carter turned her head. "How'd you know there was a but coming?"

Rusty shrugged. "You wouldn't need to talk if there wasn't a but to that statement."

"I guess not." Carter released another long sigh. "But… Jonas might be a hardass, but I love working for him. I love what his firm is doing. Brian's life is tied to his ranch close to here, but what if my future isn't meant for that? If I marry Brian…" She shook her head and fell into silence.

Rusty waited.

"Have you ever had to make an impossible choice?" Carter asked.

Obviously Rusty couldn't tell her the truth about her marriage to Will. But still, she could share some of it.

"My dad wanted to give the ranch to a man rather than to me. I had to decide to walk away from my inheritance and the ranch that is my entire life."

"Oh, wow." Carter's eyes went wide. "That had to be so hard for you."

"He's not an easy man, my father. But, in the end, walking away was the best choice for me because I needed to put my own independence ahead of keeping my dream."

Carter shook her head. "So you're saying I have to pick."

Rusty shrugged. "If you don't see a way to blend the two lives, then yes. But have you considered other options?

Maybe talked to Jonas about a way to do both? I'm sure he doesn't want to lose you. There can't be that many people in your field."

Carter pursed her lips thoughtfully. "I hadn't thought of that. He wants us in the office all the time, but I bring a skill set that's hard to find. Maybe he might…"

She shifted her gaze, suddenly focusing on Rusty. "Thank you. I needed to have that perspective change."

"If you don't like the choices, always try to change them first."

"That sounds like a quote from someone," Carter commented as she rose from the chair.

"My father says it actually." Rusty hadn't even thought of that until it came from her mouth. Funny how things turned out.

"Rusty?" Will's voice sounded from inside the house. The click of the door opening heralded his arrival. "Are you out here, honey?"

Rusty leaned forward to glance around the chair and wave. But Will had stopped walking when he saw Carter. "Baby sister!"

He swept her up in a bear hug that lifted Carter's feet from the cement floor of the porch. "About time you showed your face around here," he grumbled with a good-natured grin as he set her back down.

Carter shoved at his shoulder. "I'm here more than ever lately, but you're never around."

Will lifted a single eyebrow. "Do I need to have a serious talk with Brian? Check his intentions."

Carter sent Rusty a hesitant glance, then shrugged noncommittally. "I'm pretty sure his intentions are honorable."

Rusty got the message. Carter would look into those other options they'd discussed. She'd share with her family when she was ready.

"Good to hear," Will said, glancing between them.

Carter grabbed her suitcase and headed inside. "Let's catch up more later, okay?" she said over her shoulder.

"Sounds good." Will turned to face Rusty. "What was that about?"

"What?" she asked, widening her eyes in innocence.

"You and Carter." He thumbed toward the door through which his sister had disappeared. "Were you out here talking long?"

"Not really. She just arrived."

"Uh-huh." He eyed her speculatively for a second. "Something's going on. Something about you makes people unburden."

Rusty rolled her eyes. "If I'm the kettle then I'm looking at the pot."

"What?" he frowned.

"Your family comes to you with every problem they have." Had he not really noticed?

"No, they don't." He waved off her comment.

"Huh," she scoffed. "Take today. Autry wanted to talk to

you about a breeding decision. Jennings wanted your input on that surprise party for Cash's birthday that he's supposedly organizing but you've made all the decisions and arrangements. Cash called and got you talking about Sophia's schooling and if he should consider bumping her up a grade level."

"That's just family stuff." He really didn't see it. Williams Hill was the strong backbone of this family, and he had no idea.

"I laid all my troubles at your feet. And I don't do that. Ever." When it looked as though he'd wave that off too, she shook her head. "With anyone. But I trusted you, Will. Even when I hardly knew you."

He held up both hands. "Okay. I'm a helpful guy, I guess—"

Rusty gave a sharp nod. "And don't you forget it."

"Just like you. Carter is not a confider either, and she met you five minutes ago."

"I'm a neutral party around here is all."

"Hardly that. You've fit in here like you were made to be here."

Her heart tripped over itself at those words. Sweet words. Terrifying words. She was meant to be at Rising Star.

"What'd Carter have to say?" he asked.

Rusty fell back on the only thing she knew would keep him at a distance. Irritation. She stood and scowled at him, hands on her hips. "None of your business, Will Hill."

Will's smile had dropped when she glared, but the second she used the name combo he hated, his brows lowered. Rusty waited for him to snap her head off or try to argue with her.

But after a second, his expression cleared. "You're right. It is none of my business."

Rusty honestly had no clue how to respond to his reaction. Anger and blustering she could handle, she'd handled all her life. Reasonable… that was totally Will, she had to admit, but also out of her wheelhouse.

"Well… okay then." She dropped her hands to her sides. Hard to keep up her angry posture when he'd just taken all the wind out of her sails.

"Okay." He held out his hand, obviously for her to take.

She glanced at it, but didn't move. Touching Will was dangerous. "What?"

His mouth kicked up in a half-smile. "Escorting you inside. Mom made her famous Texas sheet cake for dessert."

Rusty straightened. "Chocolate?" she asked.

"Yup. With the best fudge icing you'll ever taste."

She put her hand in his, letting herself enjoy the strength and warmth of his grip for a heartbeat. "Lead on."

He chuckled. "You and that sweet tooth."

She took a step forward, only Will half turned and used the grip on her hand to tug her up against him. She gasped as she found herself up against his hard chest. Before she could speak, he lowered his head and claimed her lips in a long, lazy kiss. As unexpected as the action was, she had no time to slam up her walls, and sank into him with a whimper. Will took his time, exploring her mouth with leisurely care that had her hot and panting in seconds.

Finally, he lifted his head, his blue eyes smiling down at her.

Rusty licked her lips. "What was that for?" she asked, her voice coming out hoarser than she would've liked.

"Let's just say that was my dessert."

He spun away, though he took her hand again, tugging her along with him, into the house where sounds of his family spilled out into the night.

WILL LED RUSTY into the house and did his best not to strut as they went, because that kiss and the way she'd melted against him had him walking on a bubble air. Or at least that was the way it felt to him. He knew better than to take her reaction too seriously, not after the pond incident a month ago, but still.

Plus, there was the moment he'd caught between her and Carter. It had been obvious the two women had shared something, and he was busting with curiosity as to what, though he suspected it had to do with Brian. The significant part was that, of his siblings, Carter was the most private. She came off like an extrovert, and loved to meddle in other people's lives, but when it came to her private life, she tended to be closed-mouthed. Carter sharing something with Rusty meant a lot to Will.

That his wife fit in with his family was important to them. Rusty did, and that was when she was holding back. She hadn't said so, but she was. Imagine how she'd get on when she let down the walls she'd erected around her heart and let him and his family in.

"Hey, Ruthie," Autry called out as they joined everyone else in the kitchen. "Come meet Carter."

"We met outside," Rusty said, and the two women shared a smile.

"In that case, come try some of Mom's cake," Jennings said. "Your sweet tooth is going to love it."

"I love how everyone offers Rusty stuff," Will groused as Jennings handed Rusty a plate. "Where's mine?"

"You've had Mom's cake before," Jennings pointed out.

"And you've known Carter all your life," Autry said. "No need to introduce you."

"Plus, she's cuter than you, Son," his dad said, grinning around a bite of cake.

Will laughed and shook his head. "I can't argue with that. But it wouldn't hurt to feel special once in a while, too."

"You're special to me," Rusty said beside him, softly.

He turned his head to find her watching him with wide eyes, her cheeks a little pink, as though she was surprised she'd said that. Then she seemed to shake herself out of it and smiled. She scooped up a bite of cake.

"Here," she offered. "Special cake for a special guy."

It was obvious, at least to him, that whatever she'd meant by that first statement, she was rallying to put on a show for his family now. Only he didn't want to put on a show, because this was all too real to him.

Will kept his gaze on hers as he ate off her fork, the rich chocolate of the dessert barely registering over the way her pupils dilated slightly and her pink cheeks got pinker and what that did to his own body.

"Thank you, darlin'." He leaned forward to whisper in her ear. "But your kisses are much sweeter."

"Get a room," Autry interrupted loudly.

"Autry Hill, I swear." His mom huffed.

"Oh, that's right… you already have a room." Autry waggled his eyebrows, completely unrepentant.

Beside him, Rusty laughed. "You're shameless." She tossed her napkin at his brother, who caught it and popped it in the trash bin.

Will had to hold himself back from taking her by the shoulders and making a point. He wanted to say, "See. You belong in this family. You belong to me."

Only he couldn't do that. Rusty might have settled in, but she was still wary, distant. This was still a temporary thing for her. Even on the front porch when she'd pointed out her talk with Carter was none of his business, he could tell she was waiting for him to get angry and argue. The way she'd sort of shrunk in on herself had been a dead giveaway. Hadn't she figured out that wasn't his way? When would she learn to trust him? Really trust him?

Get a grip. It's been two months since you met the girl. Give her some time.

But it sure had felt like longer. He felt as though he'd known her his entire life. His life before she showed up at the rodeo in Estes Park had just been… waiting.

"Hey, where is everyone?" Cash's voice sounded from the front foyer.

"Kitchen," Will called out, along with his mother, brothers, and Carter.

A few seconds later, Sophia rushed in going straight to her grandmother for a hug first then rushed to Rusty followed by Carter. Yet another sign of how well his wife fit into his family, into his life. His heart had been right that night at the bar when he'd kissed her and fallen like a two-ton boulder.

Cash and Holly appeared more slowly, both smiling widely as they found the entire family gathered in one place.

Will glanced at Rusty, whose expression clearly said she thought the way they gathered together like this was strange. But strange good or strange bad he couldn't quite tell.

"What are you doing here?" Evaline asked around Sophia.

"We heard Carter was in town," Cash said.

John crossed his arms. "She just got here, so there's no way you heard from us."

Cash moved to the island where he'd sited his mother's cake. "We bumped into Brian."

All eyes swung Carter's way.

Carter tossed her hands up. "I have to go past his ranch on my way here. It seemed efficient to see him first."

Evaline patted her arm.

"How are things going with ol' Brian?" Will asked.

Carter glanced at Rusty, then shrugged. "About how you'd expect I guess."

"Oh, so you're getting married soon then?" Will commented offhandedly.

He didn't expect Carter to aim a scowl at Rusty who sort of scooted behind Will's shoulder even as she shook her head. Will had no trouble interpreting that byplay as evidence that a proposal was exactly what Carter had discussed with Rusty, and Will's comment made her think Rusty'd spilled to him.

Apparently, that was obvious to everyone else as well, because the entire room burst with the sound of their questions and congratulations.

Carter stuttered for a bit, but finally held up both hands. "I haven't said yes, yet," she announced.

Quiet descended over the room. The silence allowing the sounds of the crickets outside to penetrate.

Again, Carter glared Rusty's way. "I can't believe you

told—"

Rusty's chin came up. "I didn't—"

"She didn't tell me anything." Will jumped in to defend his wife. "I was teasing. Your reaction made it obvious."

"Oh," Carter huffed. Her cheeks went red. "Sorry, Rusty," she murmured.

Rusty's shoulders relaxed after a second. "It's okay. I would've thought the same thing if I were you."

The two women smiled, their expressions tinged with relief and a bit of embarrassment on Carter's side. Will wrapped an arm around Rusty's waist and pulled her into his side, dropping a kiss on the top of her head.

She stiffened at first, and even subtly tugged to get him to release her, but he waited her out, and eventually she settled against him. Right where he wanted her.

"So, he has proposed?" Evaline asked.

Carter nodded.

"Then what's the holdup? Brian's the best," Jennings said as he sliced another square of cake for himself.

Carter grimaced. "It's complicated with my career. But…" She glanced at Rusty again. "I'm going to see if working mostly remotely from the ranch is possible."

"You'd say no because of your career?" Autry asked, his tone obviously indicating his thoughts on that.

Rusty sucked in a sharp breath, but Will only knew that because of the way he held her.

Before Carter could respond, Cash jumped in to defend

his twin. "Not everyone is into the ranching life, little brother. And Carter's worked damn hard and spent a lot of money on those degrees. It'd be a shame to waste all that."

Their parents nodded in agreement. In his arms, Rusty relaxed again, giving her head a little shake.

Will leaned forward. "What?"

She angled her head to glance back at him. "Nothing."

He let her turn back to the conversation, but planned to bring it up later, because he had a feeling he knew what she'd been thinking.

"I'll tell y'all what I decide when I figure it out myself," Carter said.

"Take your time, honey." Evaline pulled her daughter in for a hug. "But congrats just the same."

At the same time, John reached out and squeezed Carter's arm, giving his own silent support.

"Is Aunt Carter getting married?" Sophia demanded, looking between the adults with a confused frown.

"Not yet, munchkin." Autry ruffled her hair.

"Good. Then we can tell you our secret now!" Sophia bounced over to her parents. Holly and Cash smiled.

"News?" Evaline asked. "Have you found out the sex?"

"Yes, and something else that we hadn't shared yet," Cash said.

"What else—" Evaline cut herself off with a gasp, her eyes wide.

Everyone else stared, not following.

"Do you want to tell them Soph?" Cash asked.

"I'm going to have a brother… and a sister!" Sophia's blond curls trembled in her excitement as she clapped and hopped up and down.

"Twins!" Will exclaimed, the first to come out of his shock.

He let go of Rusty to shake Cash's hand. "Congrats, man."

Everyone else recovered, filling the room with congrats and shared hugs.

Will pulled Holly, who was glowing with happiness, in for a hug. "That's fantastic news."

"It is wonderful news." Rusty joined them, giving Holly a hug as well.

Holly grimaced. "We're thrilled, of course. We knew at the first appointment, but wanted to wait until we were pretty far along to share that part, just in case. But now it feels more real. Two at once…" She gave a bit of a shell-shocked laugh. "I'm terrified."

He laughed. "I get that. But you have us."

Rusty turned her head sharply, giving him a searching look. Will raised his eyebrows in question, but she shook her head at him.

Holly didn't seem to notice. "I know," she said. "The family's support is the only thing keeping me sane right now."

Cash wrapped an arm around Holly, giving her a supportive squeeze. "Mom and Dad are experts at twins. We'll have plenty of help."

Again, Will got the feeling Rusty was watching all of this with a giant question mark hovering over her head. He was sure no one else caught that, but the vibe she gave off had him wondering.

The next day was Saturday, but a ranch didn't sleep in on weekends, so they didn't linger much longer, everyone heading to their respective rooms. Carter wasn't heading back to Austin until Monday, and Cash and Holly agreed to stay the weekend as well. So they'd spend more time together tomorrow.

In their room, Will waited until he and Rusty had both finished getting ready and lay in bed. "What were you thinking when Cash and Holly announced the twins?"

She glanced up from her e-reader—her nightly excuse to ignore him. "I'm thrilled for them," she said as though that should've been obvious.

"No. I mean you looked surprised about what I said concerning helping them out."

"Oh. I wasn't… surprised… exactly. More like your family is a total mystery to me."

"How's that?"

Breath hissed through her teeth and she didn't say anything for a long moment. "Your family is like the Cleavers. No one is that perfect."

She'd said that before. "Of course, we're not perfect. But

we care about each other. Something I think you've never learned about."

"I care about people," she snapped.

"That's not what I'm saying. Why are you getting mad at me?" he prodded.

She tossed him an annoyed frown. "I'm not."

"Yes, you are." He called her bluff.

"Lord, you're annoying," she muttered.

Will chuckled. "Why? Because I see things you don't want me to."

Wrong thing to say. Her lips went flat. "Because you think you do. But you don't know me, Williams Hill."

No way was he letting her get away with putting that kind of wall between them. He might not be making much forward progress, but he'd be damned if they went backward. "Yes. I do."

She rolled her eyes. "You've barely known me even two months. How could you?"

"Maybe because I pay attention," he insisted.

"Ha."

Will reached over to gently take her by the chin, turning her head to face him. "I pay attention because I *want* to pay attention, Rusty. Haven't you thought of that?"

She still didn't believe him. He could tell by the way she pulled out of his grip and tipped her chin up higher, facing him down.

"Nope," she said.

Will had no clue how to respond to that sort of stubborn refusal to listen, to see he meant what he said.

"I guess I can't argue with someone who doesn't want to hear it." He flipped over to his side, putting his back to her. At a complete loss, his only option was to get over his own annoyance, regroup, and try a different tack tomorrow. "Good night, Rusty."

Or was it time to call uncle? His heart ached at the mere thought of letting her go.

Chapter Twelve

Rusty stared at Will's back for a long couple of minutes with no idea how to respond. With a sigh, she turned off the bedside light and laid down. But she couldn't seem to get past the fact that the most open, easygoing man in the world was pissed at her.

Sure, she was always shoving him away, but he'd never once gotten angry or upset about it. At least... not like this.

She swallowed around the lump that formed in her throat. Will had turned his back on her. She'd never thought she'd annoy him enough to do that. Worse, part of her longed to hear what he had to say. That he wanted to pay attention to her. Did that mean he wanted more than this sham of a marriage?

She gave herself a shake, trying to return to reality where things like that only happened to fairy-tale princesses. Still, she hated they were going to bed with him mad at her. Not that he'd sounded mad, but this was Will. Despite her own scoffing a moment ago, she knew this man. He was ticked.

"Like what?" The words popped out of her mouth before she consciously decided to voice them.

The sheets rustled as Will shifted to look over his shoulder. "What?"

No time to wimp out now. "You said you pay attention. To what? What do you think you know about me?"

He stared at her for long moment, and she wondered if he was going to ignore her and go back to trying to sleep.

But he didn't. Something tight in her chest loosened as he rolled over to face her. Despite the lights being off, the full moon illuminated the room through the blinds and she could see his expression. Earnest now, like he wanted her to believe what he had to say.

"Will you listen and actually hear me?" he asked.

"I'll try." The damn lump in her throat just wouldn't go away.

"Okay." He seemed to think for a while.

She couldn't help but smile. "Is it that hard?"

He chuckled. "No. I'm trying to decide what I think you'll be open to hearing."

As if she was this closed-off person who was hard to communicate with? Which, if she was honest, she totally could be. She'd had her heart trampled on too many times to just put it out there. Rusty gave a mental wince. Perhaps she'd held back too much with Will, but that was self-defense for what would eventually have to end, and the fact she was already a tiny bit in love with the guy. Way too risky...

"Don't get mad," he said.

"I'm not," she lied. Granted, she had to school her face from a scowl to what she hoped was a more open expression.

He snorted. "Okay. How about this… I know you're irritated when this little crease appears between your eyebrows." He lifted a hand to trace the spot in a whisper of a touch, and Rusty sucked in a breath at the contact. And the words.

"And…" he continued, "I know you're really mad when you do that and won't look at me at the same time."

The low, deep tone he was using, like he would with a spooked horse, was messing with her breathing. Lungs that usually functioned fine had apparently given up.

"Not enough?" Will asked when she didn't speak. "Okay… more. I know the woman I met singing at a traffic light is a genius at math and horses."

An unexpected laugh popped out of her. "I wasn't sure you recognized me."

"I did."

She shivered. "Okay, horses I get. But math?"

He nodded. "Remember helping me with my books the other day?"

"Yeah." So what? She wanted to say.

"You did all the math in your head. I checked. It was right."

"Huh. And that's impressive?" she asked.

"To a guy who hated math? Yeah."

"Well, that doesn't sound very intuitive about me," she

pointed out.

"Damn. My next one was going to be that the woman I proposed to is very helpful. Anytime she sees that something needs to be done or someone who needs help, she steps in."

She giggled and shook her head, even though the fact he'd noticed something nice about her gave her a glow of warmth. "Nope. That doesn't count either."

He gave a dramatic sigh that made her want to giggle again. "I figured. Okay." He pretended to think, making a big deal of running his hand over his jaw, the rasp of his day-old beard against his skin loud in the room.

"I know the woman I married thinks it's not normal for family to be close and support each other."

"Given that I just called you the Cleavers, that's not hard to—"

He put a finger over her lips, silencing her. "You get this sort of dazed look in your eyes, and sometimes I think you'd like to join in the fun, but other times it seems like you want to run and hide from it. Do you?"

Will was being brave enough to be honest with her, she could only do the same. She pulled back from his touch. "A little."

"Why?"

She shrugged, unable to share. She wanted to be part of it, let herself be enveloped by this warm and caring group of people, but it was only temporary. Will originally married her to help his business, and she married him to get Rising

Star, even if attraction was making itself felt between them. Even if he and his family showed her what nice really was.

He let it go. "Okay. One more."

Some contrary part of her didn't want it to end, these nice things he was saying, as though he admired her. As though he saw something special in her.

"My wife is the most beautiful thing I've ever seen."

Oh my. Rusty's heart pinged around inside her chest at the words and the way his voice had gone all intense and dark.

She licked her lips. "You mean on a horse."

"No." He ran a knuckle down her cheek. "I mean period. Inside and out."

Rusty glanced away. "Now you're just teasing."

"Darlin', look at me."

She glanced up and caught her breath at the burning hunger he let her see in his eyes. He looked at her with an intensity, a possessiveness, she'd never seen before.

Every part of her throbbed in direct response to such a look, strained toward him.

"Go out with me?"

She slowly blinked, not expecting that comment. "You… want to go on a date?"

He took her face between his hands. "I want to spend time with you."

"In my bed you mean." Why was she pulling away?

The heat sparking between them was tangible, real. Even

she could feel that. And she knew this wasn't merely lust that could be slaked by a quickie in the barn.

Will kissed her, short and sweet, before pulling back again. "I won't deny that's part of the plan. But not all of it. I'm not a wham-bam-thank-you-ma'am kind of guy, Rusty. But I also want our first time to be special—and not where we have to worry about my entire family hearing."

First time. Special. The words set off little explosions of happiness inside her, like sparklers lighting her up. Every part of her wanted to say yes, but, was she setting herself up for heartbreak when this ended? Because a marriage that started the way theirs had couldn't work out, even if Will was the greatest thing since sliced bread. She hadn't picked Will, and he hadn't picked her. They'd been thrown together. The important end goal was Rising Star and Will's business.

But the chance to be a little more… more than the in-between, sort-of-friends thing they'd had going… was too much to completely ignore. Maybe a temporary slice of heaven was better than none at all?

She bit her lip. "What did you have in mind?"

"Put on shoes, then meet me out front." Will threw back the covers and started pulling on clothes, hopping about in a hurry.

Rusty couldn't help but laugh—though it came from a combination of shock and amusement and excitement all rolled into one indecipherable bubble of emotion.

Excitement and a need to see what Will had in store for them overrode all her natural instincts to keep her walls up. She wanted him. It was as simple as that.

Forty-five minutes later, she stepped out of his truck into a magical world of the Texas Hill Country on a rare cool autumn evening. She'd sat through the drive on edge with need, her hand in Will's and her body aching more with every minute of anticipation, undeterred by the bumps along the dusty track. Then they'd gone where no roads wound.

I can't believe I'm here.

Rusty watched as Will set up what she should be thinking of as a mobile one-night stand, but what honestly was stacking up to be the most romantic night of her life.

He'd packed the truck damn fast as it hadn't taken her long to pull on shoes and follow him outside. He'd kissed her, too, fast and hard, before bustling her into the truck and driving her across the ranch to a hilltop that overlooked the rolling hills.

A full moon lit the landscape, casting it in navys and blacks and silvers. Will lowered the gate and got to work. While she watched, he used a motor to blow up a mattress which took up almost the entire bed. Then he'd made it up with sheets and pillows and blankets, followed by a tent that affixed to the sides. Their own, private personal bedroom where, any second now…

Heat pooled low in her belly at the mental pictures running through her mind. Only she was so dang nervous. She wasn't a virgin. Another rebellion against her father's strict upbringing more than an act of teen love. But she was also picky and wary, so men had been few and far between in her life, and none of them got her heart pounding like the man she married.

He turned to her and must've caught her expression, because his face softened.

He stepped right into her, taking both her hands in his. "If you're not ready, we can snuggle. Talk."

Why that offer to slow things down sped things up for her, Rusty had no idea. She released one of his hands so she could put hers on his cheek, relishing the fact that she could let herself touch him this way. "You are a good man, Will."

He leaned into her touch. "Good as in the friend-zone. Or good as in something more."

"More," she whispered. "Definitely more. I don't want to just snuggle."

The breath punched from his lungs, and he scooped her up into his arms, planting a hard, possessive kiss on her lips before drawing back. "Thank God, because I would've waited, but it would've been the hardest thing I've ever done."

Rusty couldn't stop the happy giggle that escaped her. "No pun intended."

He laughed as he lifted her up and deposited her on the mattress. "That would've been hard too."

Rusty kicked off her shoes and scooted back, her heart

picking up speed as Will climbed up onto the mattress and crawled toward her, the intense, hungry expression back in his eyes.

He settled on top of her, his weight welcome and pressing her into the mattress, adding to the feel of his lips against hers. He took her lips in an urgent kiss, immediately asking for her total surrender, which she gave willingly, opening for him.

He swept his tongue over her lips to tangle with hers and she moaned low as sensations pulsed through her. Rusty swept her hands up over the hard planes of his chest and around to his back where she tugged at his shirt.

Will sat up to yank it over his head and went to gather her in his arms again, only she stopped him. "Wait."

"What?" His breathing was labored, as if he'd been running hard.

She grinned. "Give me a second to touch."

With that she ran her hands over his pecs, exploring the warmth of the skin, the hard muscles underneath, honed from years of hard ranch work. Will's jaw clenched, but he sat back, letting her touch all she wanted. She trailed her fingertips over each ridge of his stomach. But when she got to the top of his boxers, he grabbed her wrist.

"What?" she asked.

Will dropped his head, burying his face in the crook of her neck. "Honey, if you keep going like that, I won't make it to the best part."

"Oh," she breathed.

A sense of empowerment rolled over her that she could turn him on that much with a simple touch.

He dragged his lips along her neck to her collarbone and she closed her eyes, letting the sensations build with his touch. With a grunt, he snagged the bottom of her tank top, and she levered up, helping him pull it off.

He stared down at her, his face tight with need and, if she wasn't mistaken, awe, as he gazed at her body.

"God, you're beautiful, honey."

He dropped his head and took a straining nipple into the warm, wet heat of his mouth. She speared her hands through his silky hair and arched up into him.

With a groan, he gently tugged at her nipple with his teeth, drawing a shudder from her body. A moist heat gathered at her core. But he wasn't done, shifting his attention to her other breast to do the same.

"Oh. Oh. Oh." Rusty hummed her excitement, even as she held his mouth to her. "Will, that feels so good."

"You feel so good, honey." He lifted his head to smile down at her. "I don't know that I can take it slow, even though I want to. I've been waiting too long. I need you too much."

The tension radiated from his stiffly held muscles to the way he shook slightly, holding himself back.

"Me too," she husked. "Slow is overrated."

Will laughed and shook his head, marveling at the woman in his arms. Finally in his arms. She was glorious. Her responses, her kisses, the way she'd touched him like she wanted to memorize his body. He couldn't get enough of her.

His throbbing dick demanded action. With another grin, Will tackled her shorts and panties, hampered by her hands trying to get at his shorts.

Somehow, between the two of them, they ended up naked. Will reached for the stash of condoms he'd made sure to bring. No repeat of the pond situation. With hands shaking slightly from the blood pumping through his body, he rolled it on. Then he moved over her again, to settle between her legs.

Her sweet warmth drove him crazy and he had to kiss her. He cupped her breast, pausing to tweak her nipple and loving her indrawn gasp, then smoothing over the dip of her waist, the curve of her hip, and the smooth skin of her thigh. He hooked his hand behind her knee and drew her leg wider, giving his body better access.

Then he went up on one elbow and watched her face as he found her hot, moist center. Her lips parted in silent need as he brushed his thumb over the bundle of nerves hidden in her slick folds.

Slowly, torturing himself as much as her, he slid a single

finger inside her. She was ready for him, but he wanted this to be as perfect for her as it already was for him. He found her clit with his thumb again, and with tandem movements, pumped his finger into her while pressing and circling that spot guaranteed to drive her body higher.

He drank in the sight of her—red curls spilling over the white of his pillow, pert breasts rising and falling with each breath, ripe lips parted as she panted in time to his pumping fingers.

"You are so beautiful."

Her eyes snapped open then widened slightly as she caught his stare. "You… are… too…" she got out between breaths. Then she moaned as he pressed a little harder with his thumb.

"I'm so close," she said.

He could tell, as her hips started to buck under his touch.

Will pulled his hand away.

"Don't stop," she begged.

"Don't worry, honey. I'm not."

He took his cock in hand and lined up with her entrance, then pushed slowly, slowly inside her, in little rocking motions, giving her body a chance to adjust to his until he was fully inside her.

Will paused, needing to take a moment to relish this, marvel at the feel of her around him, more exquisite than he'd ever imagined.

"Will, please," she moaned.

Everything inside him tensed and heated at her words, the hoarse sound of need in her voice. She craved this as much as he did.

Slowly, he started to move inside her, sliding in and out of her tight channel, his own low moans joining hers as the tension built inside them. He gradually increased the pace, moving faster. Wanting her to be there with him, he pulled back so he could get a hand between them, pushing against the spot that would enhance things for her.

"Rusty. Look at me, baby."

She opened her eyes and stared back at him as he moved. One more pump, one more press of his thumb and she tipped over, her face beautiful as waves of ecstasy pulsed through her. He didn't think he'd ever see anything more perfect than his wife at this moment.

The tightening of her body around his, the sounds issuing from her, pulled him under. He thickened, then his release poured from him in hot spurts. He kept moving until he'd wrung every shudder of pleasure from their orgasms.

Then he dropped, chest heaving as he caught his breath, and buried his face in her neck, inhaling her sweet rose scent.

"You slay me, honey," her murmured in her neck.

"Back at ya." She shifted underneath him, and Will realized he was probably crushing her.

He rolled to his side, and disposed of the condom, tossing it over the side of the truck out from under the tent siding, making a mental note to pick it up later to throw away.

Then he pulled Rusty into his side, tucking her head on his chest. After a long moment he dropped a kiss on the top of her head. "Please tell me you don't regret that."

Her eyelashes fluttered against his skin, then she lifted her head to look at him. "Never. I could never regret that."

Something tight inside his chest gave way and Will smiled as he traced her lips with the pad of his thumb. "Good."

Still, he didn't miss the flash of worry that entered her eyes. "What?" he asked.

Her lips pressed together and she lowered her eyes.

He tucked a strand of hair behind her ear then touched her chin, lifting her eyes to his. "Talk to me, honey, or I can't fix it."

She shook her head. "There's nothing that needs fixing. I'm just…" She sighed. "You said you want more than one night?"

"Yes."

She blinked at his swift and assured answer. "What do you mean?"

Now was Will's turn to measure his words. He ran his free hand through his hair, thinking. He'd tell her straight out if he wasn't afraid she'd run off screaming. Still she was asking. "I want you."

Nothing could be more clear than that.

But apparently that wasn't clear enough. She traced a pattern on his chest. "That sounds lovely. What does it mean?"

He blew out a long breath. "Before I explain what that means, I want you to know that there's no pressure. We can take this as slow as you need. Okay?"

"Okay." She drew out the word. The way her muscles stiffened she seemed to be readying herself for bad news.

"I don't want you to leave."

She frowned. "Leave here?"

He shook his head. "Leave me."

Her eyebrows shot up. "Because you need a good trainer now that Holly is having twins?"

Will gritted his teeth to keep from giving her a little shake. Why could she not believe he wanted her? Only her.

"No. I want you to stay as my wife. I want this marriage to be real."

There. He'd said it.

He watched her face closely as she absorbed that truth. "But you hardly know me."

At least that response didn't involve running and screaming.

He settled a bit, pulling her closer. "I think I've already proven how well I know you." If he told her he'd fallen for her the moment he saw her, she would never believe him. His wife was both practical and skeptical. Not the easiest combination to convince that sometimes love didn't ask for time.

He tucked her head onto his chest. "You don't need to answer now or say or do anything you're not ready for. But you asked. Just… just consider staying. Okay?"

She was silent long enough that he started to worry. But then she relaxed against him, pressing a kiss against his chest. "Okay."

He barely caught the whispered agreement and couldn't help his grin. He wanted to pump his fist in the air. He'd never thought he'd get even that much from her.

"And maybe, while you're thinking, we can keep doing more of this?" He waved at their naked bodies.

"Hmmm…"

He wasn't sure if that was an agreement, but it wasn't a "no" so Will closed his eyes and held her tight.

The bed jiggled as Rusty moved beside him, probably pulling up the sheet to cover up with. But then the bed shifted more, and suddenly he felt her weight as she lifted over him.

Will jerked his eyes open to find Rusty straddling him, the sight of her naked and the feel of her above him had him hardening in anticipation, even as he tried to put on the brakes.

"I didn't mean right now," he said. "I understand if you need time to think about—"

She reached out and put her finger against his lips, silencing him.

She smiled, and his cock twitched as she rubbed against him intimately. "I'm taking advantage of you."

"Are you sure…"

"This is me making the move, Will. No guilt for you. I want this. I want you."

He swallowed. Even as his hands dropped to her hips, he had to try one more time. "I don't want you regretting or thinking that I assume—"

Suddenly, Rusty leaned forward and placed her lips over his, effectively silencing him.

After a moment, she lifted her head, only enough to murmur against his lips. "You think too much."

Chapter Thirteen

WILL GRIPPED THE phone as he listened to the rodeo organizer talking on the other end. "What do you mean you don't need my bulls?" he demanded. "The Turtle is the top performing bull in the circuit right now, and several others are up there as well."

"Sorry, Mr. Hill, but we're a small rodeo and usually only have one stock contractor. Turns out, we have enough with the bulls they're providing."

Will let out a long breath. Dammit, he could've used the money Turtle was bringing him. Still, this was the business. The rodeo venue could ask whoever they wanted. "I understand. I hope you'll think of us next year."

"Of course." Then the organizer hung up.

Which basically meant they wouldn't be invited next year either.

Will put down his cell phone and ran a hand round the back of his neck. "Dammit."

"Problem?"

He jerked his head up to find Rusty standing in his open doorway, hand raised to knock.

She was dressed in her usual attire—jeans, shirt, boots. Nothing crazy. But he knew what lay under those clothes now. He did his best not to drag her inside his office and shut the door, instead shaking his head. "The rodeo we were scheduled for in two weeks just cancelled on me."

"Why?" She moved inside to plonk down on the chair across from his desk.

"Said they had enough with their usual contractor."

Rusty didn't move, but she'd frozen in place. "Which rodeo?" she asked slowly.

"The Heartland Rodeo in Colorado."

Her lips pinched so hard they went white. "They didn't *just* cancel on you," she said.

A sinking sensation moved from his chest to his toes. "Don't tell me…"

"Rising Star is the sole contractor for that rodeo. Has been for going on twenty years now."

Will dropped back in his chair as the implications struck. "You're not suggesting your father had me kicked out of the lineup. Why would he do that to his son-in-law?"

She nibbled at her bottom lip in the most distracting way. "I guess he doesn't believe us."

Will choked on that statement. "We haven't even visited him yet. He was at our wedding for Pete's sake. Why wouldn't he believe us?"

"The Turtle is the top ranked bull on the circuit right now, so that rodeo only canceled if they had pressure. Can you think of a better explanation? He must want something else."

"Like what? A contract signed in blood?" How had she dealt with this crap for so long?

"I don't know. Some kind of proof that makes sense in the land of crazy." She jumped to her feet, pacing back and forth in the small space in front of his desk. "I can't believe he'd mess with your business. What on earth could he—"

She turned to Will, her eyes narrowed, suspicion radiating from her, and leaned both hands on his desk. "How are the partnership discussions with my father going, Will? I haven't heard much along those lines."

He raised his eyebrows. "It hasn't gone anywhere. I told you I'd only partner with you, and I meant it."

"Dammit." She flung her arms wide. "Why didn't you tell me?"

"I did tell you when I proposed. Plus, you said you didn't want to be involved. I don't see what my wanting to only partner with you has to do with this."

"He won't see it that way. To him, the business is separate. You backed out."

"And he'd punish me for that when I'm married to his daughter?"

"I can't think of anything else." She resumed pacing the room, only now she was muttering to herself. Something about "on her own" and "no stock contractors." However, when he caught the words "find a replacement," Will jumped to his feet.

"Whoa, whoa, whoa," he said. "What are you thinking?"

"I'm not letting my family fight affect your business, Will. That's not fair to you."

"No." He came around the desk and took her by the shoulders. "First of all, we don't know if you're right."

She stared up at him, chin jutted out, not giving an inch. "Even if that's not the reason, it's something else."

"Regardless, leaving here is *not* the answer."

"It's the only answer. I'll have to start my own business outside of a ranch, so it's only me. Then he can't hurt anyone else."

"With what money? You'll need to stable the horses, feed them, a place to train them," he pointed out.

She twitched under his hands. "I know. I'll figure it out."

"There's got to be a better answer."

She stepped back, and he dropped his hands to his sides.

"There is none," she snapped.

There was no arguing her out of it. As much as she tried to hide it, Rusty had a heart as big as Texas, and no way would she let people she cared about get hurt if she could help it.

That he fell into that category—people she cared about—gave him a buzz of satisfaction. But at the moment, the buzz was overridden by bone-deep fear she'd follow through on leaving him in order to help him.

Will shook his head. "I'm not letting you leave me. Not

after what we've shared."

Rusty swallowed hard, but at least she didn't keep arguing.

He took her hand, halting her pacing. "How about this. Our first trip out to see him is next week. No major decisions until we have a chance to get a better idea of what he's up to."

She sighed. "I won't leave yet, but a week or two is all I'm willing to wait. I'm telling you, he wants something else and going after you is how he intends to get it."

"You don't leave without talking to me first though. Agreed?"

"Agreed."

The tightness in his chest eased a fraction. "Okay."

"What's your lineup of rodeos coming up?" she asked.

Will knew where she was going with this.

He rounded his desk and punched up the schedule on his computer. Rusty came around to watch over his shoulder, her body brushing up against his.

"There." She pointed. "Rising Star is the major stock contractor for this rodeo in October. If he gets them to cancel, then we know he's still after something."

He turned to lean against his desk, facing her, with a shake of his head. "What's his motivation?"

She shrugged. "On top of being good business to ensure he's the kingpin in the area, he knows coming after me with whatever he wants won't work. I'm too stubborn. But if he undermines my job or my husband…"

"He forces you to agree?" Could her father be that much of an asshole?

She nodded. "At least in his head, the end justifies the means. Dad had zero concept of how to deal with raising a girl. When I was little, he treated me like a boy. Short hair, boy clothing, learn to rope and ride. But then I grew up. His reaction was to try to control everything."

"Bet you loved that," Will muttered.

"You could say the apple doesn't fall far from the tree in the pig-headed department in our family." She traced a crack in the top of his well-worn desk. "He got worse after Reed died," she murmured softly.

"Probably doesn't help that you look like you do."

Wide brown eyes stared back at him. "Why Williams Aaron Hill…" She batted her eyelashes. "What a thing to say."

He crossed his arms to keep from reaching for her. "Who told you my middle name?"

"Your mother. She seems to think I want to know everything about you. I've even see that picture of you running around with only boots on. What a cute butt…" She grinned.

He knew the picture. He wasn't more than two years old in it. When she got like this, hiding a vulnerability with banter, he just wanted to kiss her until she let him in.

Instead, he played along. "Maybe I should ask your father to send baby pictures of your butt. To even us out."

She snorted. "Good luck with that."

He hummed his agreement. "I'm starting to realize why your father wanted to keep you under lock and key."

She frowned her confusion. "Oh?"

"I'm having a hard time keeping my hands off you."

Her eyes went wide, then she smirked. "You've been taking flirting lessons from Autry?"

But he wasn't ready to let up yet. "What can I say, ma'am..." He used his thickest Southern drawl. "You rival the stars."

She rolled her eyes even as her cheeks turned an adorable shade of pink. But she didn't step back or look away, and suddenly, Will didn't want to ignore the pull she had on him anymore. He wanted to give into it, like the ocean followed the moon.

He straightened and her eyes widened. Will took a step forward and Rusty took a step backward. "Will..."

He kept moving. "Rusty."

"We agreed. No hanky-panky during business hours." Their night together in his truck had led to what Will considered the best few weeks of his entire life. They worked side by side as if fate had meant them to, they enjoyed time with his family, and, at night, they enjoyed each other. No way was her father going to ruin this.

He raised his eyebrows, still teasing. "I'm just walking."

Now she shifted to glaring. "No, you're not. You have

that look."

He couldn't hold back a smile. "What look?"

"Like you want to kiss me."

"Oh, that look." He shrugged. "I want to do a whole lot more than kiss you, darlin'."

Rusty bumped up against the wall to his office and he stopped close, but not quite touching. With a small shove, he closed the door, giving them total privacy. Then, still not touching, he leaned down until his lips hovered above hers. "Tell me to walk away."

He waited while the debate raged in her expressive eyes. She wanted him, he knew she did. But her independence was important, something he got after tangling with her father in small ways. Plus, he suspected she'd been so sheltered, her experience with men was limited to keeping them at arm's length, and, until today, he hadn't brought their lovemaking out of the bedroom. But her father's actions had altered his timeline for capturing the heart of one Rusty Hill.

Her tongue darted out to wet her lower lip and he groaned. "Honey, don't do that unless you want me to repeat the action for you."

Suddenly, something gave in her eyes and her shoulders dropped a fraction. "I guess I'm a sucker for a hot cowboy who stares at me like I'm the most precious thing in the world."

Will opened his mouth to reply, but Rusty took over, going up on tiptoe to claim his lips, sweeping her tongue across his mouth in the way he'd just threatened to do to her. Tension that had been building ever since he'd let her out of his bed this morning, hell, ever since the first time he'd seen her ride Mischief, exploded between them.

In an instant, he was hard and aching and urgent. And Rusty's frantic hands, the way she pressed her body against his like she couldn't get close enough, had him lost, adrift at sea… and loving it.

He dragged his lips away from hers. "I need you."

"I know. Me too." She was panting, her eyes dark and slumberous, lips wet and raw from his kisses. "Good thing you have a lock on your door and a couch in here."

The air punched from his lungs. "You are going to kill me, woman."

But he grinned as he reached for the lock on the door, then he yanked her back into his arms and lost himself in heaven.

TWO WEEKS AND not a peep from her father. Not even a comment about babies when she talked to him on the phone. *No way has he given up.* Rusty did her best to keep her churning suspicions at bay. Now that she was finally home she could get some answers.

"Dad?" Rusty called as she walked through the pristinely clean rustic home where she'd grown up and lived almost her entire life.

The wood floors gleamed. So did the floor-to-second-story-ceiling windows that looked out over the ranch. The house was set up on the side of a hill, built into it. This newer construction had replaced the original dwelling built a few generations back. They'd been smart, using the hill as protection from the winds and snows that could blow harshly in the winters. Her dad had seen no need to change the location. Though she missed the old house which had been smaller and cozier.

"Dad?" she called again, as she walked toward his office situated at the back of the house off the master bedroom where he wouldn't be disturbed.

Except for right now.

She checked his bedroom, which was empty, but saw the light on under his office door. Halfway across the room, she happened to glance at his dresser, and stopped in her tracks. The picture of her father and mother on their wedding day—both young and vital, her father stoic as ever, her mother glowing with happiness—was still there. She'd often snuck in here to stare at it and wonder about her mother, and what her parents had been like before.

But now, beside that picture was one of Rusty and Will. They were sharing their first kiss. The justice of the peace who married them in Cheyenne smiled indulgently behind them. Rusty had no idea this picture even existed. But why had her father framed it and put it in here?

Doris must've snapped one with her phone and put it in here for him. That could be the only explanation.

Rusty gave herself a little shake then crossed the rest of the room to knock at her father's door.

"Come in," came his gruff call.

She took a deep breath and entered. She'd only been gone a short while, but already this felt foreign. Nothing had changed. The massive oak table he used for a desk, the wingbacked leather chairs seated across from him, the large windows with a direct view of the barn. All the same. The leather and wood polish smell that she associated with this room washed over her and Rusty was back to the twelve-year-old girl whose father didn't want her.

Will had made her promise to remain calm. "Hi, Dad," she said when he didn't look up from his computer.

Irritation clawed at her until she noticed the medical-looking machine to his right, all white and silver and plastic tubes. Had he been doing his chemo treatments in here?

Faded blue eyes lifted to regard her for a long moment. "About time you came to visit."

"We told you at the wedding that this was when we'd visit. We needed to get set up at home before starting to go back and forth."

Funny how High Hill Ranch felt more like home now than Rising Star ever had.

"How are you feeling?" she asked.

She searched his weathered face for any sign of the illness

destroying his body, but he appeared much the same as always. Most of the times she'd called home since leaving, her father had been out doing ranch business or asleep. But Doris had kept her informed of his progress, so Rusty wasn't too surprised.

"So far so good. Doc thinks I'm a walking miracle. Says I should be bedridden by now."

"That's great, Dad. Maybe we get to keep you a while longer." And strangely, despite their strained relationship and his recent antics, she suddenly wanted that. She couldn't imagine Rising Star or her life without him.

He grunted in reply. "How long are you here?"

"I can't leave the horses too long. We're planning to stay for a week this time. Then we'll be back once a month for three or four days each visit."

Another grunt greeted the information. She'd already told him this once though. Was that a sign of his illness?

"Better get unpacked then," he said.

"Will is taking care of that right now."

Her father rose from his seat. "Why didn't you say so? I'd better go say hello to my son-in-law."

Huh. She had no doubts her father knew exactly when they arrived. But *she* had to come find him while the *new son* got sought out. That would've stung once upon a time, but somehow she found him predictable rather than irritating or hurtful now.

"Before you do, I have to talk to you about something."

"It can wait." He waved a dismissive hand.

"No, Dad. This can't wait." She'd already waited to confront him until they got here.

Weeks she'd waited, wondering what his new game was, dreading how she'd have to leave Will. Because she would have to, and doing so would break her heart.

"Fine. Get it said then."

Typical. "I know you blocked Will from being invited to two rodeos."

He crossed his arms, but didn't deny it.

"What are you after?"

He glared at her for a long moment, but Rusty just tipped up her chin and stared back expectantly. Be damned if she broke first.

"I'm not convinced this marriage is real," he said.

Rusty put her hands on her hips and silently reminded herself a fit on the floor wouldn't solve this issue. "You were at the wedding, Dad. It's real enough."

He shook his head. "Something about that bugged me and I couldn't put my finger on it until Doris mentioned how she thought you would've wanted more of your college friends at it."

"*You* didn't give me time for what *I* wanted," she pointed out in what she thought was an admirably reasonable tone.

"Well, I didn't mean for you to get married that weekend." A familiar edge entered his voice, one which told her this was her fault in his eyes.

"I didn't expect to meet Will," she murmured quietly.

He gave her a narrow-eyed look, as though searching for the truth. Rusty waited, because this wasn't over.

"I wouldn't put it past you to have made some deal with him to marry you and you'll end it when all is said and done."

"That does sound like me." Rusty knew better than to bluster or argue.

Her retort only earned her a glare. "I don't need your sass, young lady."

"That wasn't sass, sir. I was agreeing with you."

"This is serious business."

"I agree." Now she scowled. "When you affect my husband's business, I take that very seriously. What I can't understand is why?"

"Call it a demonstration."

Dread sank into her stomach to mix with the anger and frustration already rolling around in there. "To prove what?"

He shrugged. "What's at stake."

Here it came. "What new scheme have you cooked up?"

"Babies."

Rusty sucked in a sharp breath. "Excuse me?" she said faintly.

"I've amended things so that everything goes to any children you and Will—and only Will as the father—should have together. It'll go into a trust in their names."

Holy shit. She had not been expecting this at all. A demand that she leave Will and marry who her father designated maybe, except he seemed perfectly happy with Will in the role. Or wanting that partnership for the ranch set up with himself instead of her. But babies? Damn.

"And if we don't have children?"

He smirked. "Then everything goes to my original choice."

God, his smug smile. "Is there a time limit on this deal?"

Knowing her father, no way was he leaving this up to her timing, not that she was going to have children with Will. The thought of carrying his child made her glow, but he'd already done too much for her. He might want her, maybe even love her, but he didn't deserve to be forced into such a huge life decisions. A fake marriage was more than enough. Rusty clenched her fists at her sides as pain from that thought tore through her. In the last few weeks she'd let herself wish for a real marriage with Will—one that included family and love and children. A fantasy she'd hardly let herself believe.

Besides, one thing life had taught her was that *she* wasn't enough. Not by herself. She hadn't been enough for her father. Ever. Not as an heir, or a partner in the business, or really as his child. She hadn't been enough for those other men who only wanted what she gave them access to. What if Will decided she wasn't enough either? That would shatter her. She might put up a brave, spunky face to the world, but inside she was still that little girl who only knew rejection.

"You have six months from when the will goes into effect," her father said.

"Some couples take years to get pregnant. Have you thought of that?"

Her father shrugged. "Not Walkers. And, given how many siblings Will has, not the Hills either."

"That doesn't automatically make me a baby factory, Dad."

"I'm surprised you haven't been trying already. I mentioned this to Will at the wedding."

The entire world came to a screeching halt. Rusty wasn't sure if silence could roar or if the blood was pounding so hard through her veins that she could hear the rush.

"Will knows?" she choked out.

"Of course. I told him I expected news of my first grandbaby before the year was out."

Oh, God. Will had known all along, and he'd… Bile rose up Rusty's throat at the thought of what they'd been doing the last few weeks. The slide of suspicion oozed through her, something she couldn't ignore. Those special moments now tainted by the knowledge that it had all been a sham.

"Excuse me," she said. "I need to speak with my husband." She bit that last word out.

Rusty stalked from the room. The only thing keeping her from collapsing in a puddle of misery unable to breathe or think was anger. She held onto that anger with both hands, because the alternative devastation was something she couldn't face.

At the top of the staircase, she turned right. Her room was the last one at the end of the hall. Inside, she found Will unpacking his things from the large suitcase they'd shared for the trip up.

He spared her a quick smiling glance before returning to his task. "How'd it go?" he asked.

Rusty stood in the doorway, shaking. "He wants us to have babies."

His hands stopped moving as he absorbed that. Then he straightened, eyebrows sky high. "Really?"

She cocked her head. "I thought you already knew."

Now those brows lowered in a frown. "Knew? How would I know that?"

He was going to lie to her face? "He said he told you at the wedding."

Something in her tone must've alerted him, because Will put his hands on his hips and gave her face a closer look. "What's going through your head right now?"

She pinched her lips closed, reluctant to voice her thoughts and have them confirmed. "Dad says he told you about wanting babies at the wedding."

"Yeah? Some offhand comment I didn't take seriously. So?"

"It's part of his will. The ranch goes to our children, the first of which we have to have within six months of Dad…"

"Fuck," he muttered, running a hand round the back of his neck. "How could he—" Will broke off and jerked his gaze up to hers.

He stared at her for a long moment, seeming to assess her expression, the way she was holding herself so stiffly. "You think I knew?" he asked in a voice so quiet she had to strain to hear him.

"You just said you knew," she pointed out.

Talking was getting difficult as her throat constricted around the words and the tears threatening.

"You think I made a move on you to get you pregnant?" He'd gone even quieter now and she didn't like it.

Still, she tipped up her chin, refusing to back down, her hurt and anger and fear still too close to the surface to let her. He knew. He knew. She couldn't get around that fact.

"You think I'd do something like that?"

Not until ten minutes ago. She never would've suspected, at least not since she'd got to know him and his family, but that was what made his move so brilliant. She hadn't suspected.

"Wouldn't you?" she asked.

"Dammit, Rusty." He looked out the window, his jaw working.

She waited—for him to deny it, for him to explain, for him to argue her out of the belief. Because if it wasn't true, that was what he'd do. He cared for her, or so she'd recently started to believe. If that was real, he'd fight for her.

After what felt like a year of silence, he turned back to the suitcase. Only now, instead of unpacking, he started putting his stuff back in it and pulling out her things.

"What are you doing?" she asked.

"Leaving you." He wouldn't look at her.

Proof that she was right? Rusty sucked in a sharp breath as pain scissored through her. "I see. Got caught and now you're giving up?"

That got him to look up, and she flinched at the anger in his eyes. She realized she'd never seen Will angry, truly angry… until now.

"You've made it impossible for me no matter what. Damned if I do, damned if I don't. I fell in love with you and you just kicked that in my teeth."

Rusty's only recourse was denial. "Convenient to claim love now."

A savage look crossed his features and she'd crossed some line she hadn't realized existed.

"Send my things to me later."

With that he abandoned the suitcase, stalked past her, out of the door and out of her life.

Rusty shut her eyes tight, frozen by confusion, and fear, and pure pain. He hated her. She'd done that. She'd pushed him over some edge.

The sound of his truck starting up had her running to the window to see him flying down the dirt road that led off the ranch.

Chapter Fourteen

WILL DROVE WITHOUT much thought as to the where, angrier than he ever remembered being. Luckily, this far out, the road was a fairly simple straight shot for a while, allowing him to just go. Deliberately, he held onto his anger, because it was the only thing between him and what he suspected would be gut-wrenching misery because he'd lost her.

Hell, he'd never had her.

But until this moment, he'd allowed himself to hope. Especially the last few weeks. She'd opened up to him—not just giving her body, but he hadn't caught a single look of suspicion or wariness in her big brown eyes, and she'd seemed to settle more in with his family.

He'd been wrong.

Because no way could someone who'd learned to trust him ever think he'd do what she suspected.

Will slammed a hand into the steering wheel.

Rusty'd actually thought he'd try to get her pregnant to get his hands on Rising Star? After everything he'd tried to show her, be to her, the betrayal went soul-deep. And damn her father for breaking her spirit in such a way she'd ever have to wonder those kinds of thoughts.

I'm done.

Will clenched his jaw so tightly, pain radiated up his skull. The problem was, if he let himself continue, she'd only smash his heart. He loved her. He suspected he'd loved her since the day he met her, though that still seemed ridiculous. No matter when it started, he loved Rusty Walker Hill with every ounce of himself.

But he couldn't fix her, and trying would break him.

Will drove without purpose for hours, finding himself back at the airport in Cheyenne. But he didn't want to go home. Not yet. Not without her.

Will pulled into the parking garage and turned on his cell phone which he'd shut off. He refused to allow himself to acknowledge the disappointment that dropped into his stomach as zero messages from Rusty showed.

He searched for a number and dialed. When a female voice answered, he took a deep breath. "Do you have any rooms available?"

RUSTY LAY ON her bed, staring out the window through which she'd watched the best man she ever knew walk out of her life.

Walk? Hell, he'd skidded out of her life, dirt flying from

under his tires.

A soft rap at her door had her up. She sat and wiped an arm across her cheeks. Taking a deep breath, she crossed the room, then opened the door. Given the tentative knock, she'd expected Doris. Instead she found her father standing there.

He straightened as she opened the door, then paused, searching her face with an intent gaze.

"Is it dinnertime?" she asked.

That could be the only reason for his bothering to disturb her.

"Will's gone," he said.

Rusty crossed her arms. "Are you asking or telling me?"

His craggy face pulled into a frown. "Both. I saw him leave."

"Yes. I… ended it."

That got his attention. Her father narrowed his eyes. "Ended it?"

"Yes. You were right, of course. Our marriage was one of convenience to get around your unreasonable need to control my life. I hope you're happy, because now Rising Star will go to the man you selected and no longer be part of the Walker family."

Rusty went to close her door, but her father put out a hand stopping her.

Again, he searched her face for a long time. At least she assumed he did. She refused to look at him.

"I don't think I've ever seen you cry," he said.

She shrugged, still refusing to look up.

"Not even when Midnight threw you and you broke your arm."

She gritted her teeth. A walk down memory lane was not what she was in the mood for right now.

"Not even when your brother died." This he said softly.

She pulled her gaze up. "Oh, I cried. But Reed made me promise once, when I was young, that I'd never cry in front of you."

For the first time ever, she had the satisfaction of seeing her father flinch. But she was too heartbroken to care. She went to shut the door again, but again he stopped her.

"I know I made mistakes as your father."

Shock held her immobile.

"I had no idea how to raise a girl without your mother. Then your brother died, and I was…" He shook his head. "Not that it's an excuse."

She didn't say anything. What could she say?

"Then my body went against me with this damn cancer, and all I could see was that you were alone. That I was leaving you without anyone to care for you or help you."

"The staff and hands are all well trained, Dad. I'd have plenty of help."

He scowled, finally looking more like her father. "Shut up and listen for a minute, girl."

Rusty crossed her arms, and stared back at him, muscles

so tense she was on the edge of shaking.

Garrett Walker ran a hand through white hair that she could now see had thinned significantly since the last time she saw him. "I know what it's like to spend your life surrounded by other people, and still be completely alone. After your mother died…" He shook his head. "She left a hole in my life that no one and nothing, not even this ranch, could fill."

Except I was here. If he would've let her in. But damned if she'd say that.

"I made my own bed, especially with my children," he said, almost as though he'd read her mind. "And I have to deal with that. But I figured I could go to my grave easier if I thought I'd taken care of you."

"By taking away my home?" she snapped.

"This ranch is no place to find love. You have to find it out in the world. You're a Walker—stubborn to the end—my goal was to either make you finally go looking, or send you off into the world after I was gone, where you could find someone on your own time. Either way, you wouldn't end up like your old man." He ended the last on a gruff note.

"And the babies?"

His lips went flat. "A dumbass idea to make sure I'd done the right thing with you and Will," he muttered. "No way would you have babies if you didn't love him."

Oh. Much of the anger went out of her. Still, why was he bothering to tell her now?

He let out a long breath. "I can see that you love Will. Or you wouldn't be crying."

Rusty shook her head. "I just told you our marriage was a sham."

"Then why the tears?" he asked.

"Obviously I'm upset about losing Rising Star. I love this place."

He snorted. "Of course you do. You're my daughter. But those tears aren't for the ranch, and don't lie to me."

Now here was the man she knew. "So what if I do," she snapped. "He's gone now."

Then she sucked in a sharp breath. *I love Will.*

But of course she did. Some part of her had always known that, or she would never have said yes when he proposed. Not even to keep Rising Star. She closed her eyes as anguish welled up inside her. Now she'd lost him forever with her horrible suspicions and accusations. Of course Will hadn't played her. He was not that kind of man.

"So what are you going to do about his leaving?"

She snapped her eyes open at her father's question. "What?"

"No child of mine ever quit anything," he snapped. "Are you going to quit now? Just because it's hard?"

She blinked. "What about the ranch?"

He waved a hand. "Don't you worry about the ranch. It's yours no matter what. You just go get him back." Then he paused. "If… if that's what would make you happy."

Rusty stared at her father, seeing him a little more clearly for perhaps the first time in her life. He wasn't a monster, no matter how controlling an ass he could be. Had he only been trying to make sure he left her cared for?

Suspicion still roiled inside her. Too many years with his manipulative machinations didn't make that go away after one conversation, but she didn't voice her doubts. She'd rather believe the better of him in these last weeks and months of his life. Maybe even make amends for her own stubborn part to play. He was her father after all, and her only remaining living relative.

"I don't even know where Will went," she mumbled.

A sneaky grin snuck across his face. "I can help with that. Come on."

He led her back downstairs to his office where he punched something up on the computer. "Will took the truck I had Dave pick you up in."

"So?"

"I put a GPS tracking device in all the ranch vehicles, so I can check that people are doing their work."

Sounded exactly like something her father would do.

"Where is he?" she asked. She prayed he wasn't already flying home to Texas.

Her father clicked through until he located the truck. "Interesting spot to choose."

Rusty frowned. Why would Will be in the center of Cheyenne? Then she got a better look at the names of the cross streets and gasped.

"I know where he is," she said. Then she ran out of the room.

"Don't come back unless it's with Will," her father shouted after her.

But for once, she didn't take that as a threat and laughed. Though she sobered as she scooted behind the wheel of her father's truck. She flipped down the visor and the keys fell in her lap, then she gunned the vehicle, and took off, tires spitting up dirt and rocks behind her.

She had not one damn clue what she was going to do when she got to Will, but she had to try. An idea came to her suddenly. Her father wouldn't like it, but he could stuff it. She grabbed her cell phone and dialed.

"Dad? I need to meet with your lawyer. Right now."

WILL LAY ON top of the white bedspread on the iron bed in the room where Rusty had stayed at the Nagle-Warren Mansion. He'd been surprised both his room and her room had been available. What prompted him to take her room, he had no idea.

In fact, this walk down memory lane was pointless. But part of him felt closer to her in here. Maybe this way he could say goodbye before he went home.

Alone.

Then he had to explain everything to his family.

Arms tucked behind his head, and feet crossed at the ankles, his boots on the floor, he stared at the ceiling. He'd been here for hours, just staring. The sky had turned dark, and at some point he'd flipped on the antique lamp on the bedside table. Then he'd gone back to staring. He should probably get up and have dinner, but he couldn't make himself.

A knock at the door made him jump. Will propped himself up on one elbow. "Yes?"

No one knew he was here, so it could only be hotel staff.

"Sir," a female voice called through the door, "I have a delivery for you."

"Are you sure it's for Williams Hill?" he called back even as he scooted off the bed and moved to answer the door.

"Very sure," she answered.

He swung the door open to find the gray-haired woman who'd checked him in standing there with a manila envelope. Scrawled on the outside of it was his full name. Including his middle name. What the hell?

Slowly he reached out for it. "Thanks," he murmured, even as he turned to close the door.

Then he dug into the envelope to pull out a small stack of what appeared to be legal documents. These couldn't be for him. He went to stuff them back in, but paused as he saw his name, and one other that had him grunting.

He pulled the papers back out, skimming them quickly.

Then his frown deepened to a scowl. It appeared as though Rusty was putting her inheritance in his name, but only if he agreed to stayed married to her.

Will stalked to the door and took the stairs practically two at a time. He had no clue how she'd found him, but it didn't matter. This was a low blow, and he wasn't going to take it lying down. That was for damn sure.

He found the woman who'd brought him the papers behind the front desk. She lit up with a smile when she saw him.

Will held up the papers. "Where is the woman who brought these?"

"She's waiting for you in the dining room, sir." She pointed.

Will burst through the closed French doors, and pulled himself short at the sight of Rusty standing there. Her dress registered, even through his anger. Some kind of soft velvety material smoothed over her curves. The striking shade of blue looked incredible against her creamy skin and dark red hair. The low V-neck showed off her cleavage, even as the long sleeves and knee length gave it a buttoned-up appearance that only made her sexier.

He'd never seen her dress like this.

He gave himself a shake. Just because she looked like his idea of heaven didn't make him any less pissed.

Will held up the papers. "What the hell is this supposed to mean?"

She did a rapid blink, and her shoulders sagged. "I was hoping—"

"What? That you'd test me?"

Her head jerked back, her eyes wide. "No, that's not what I—"

"I know your father made you stop trusting men, but when have I ever given you reason to doubt me—"

"You haven't." She shook her head, her long hair, loose for once, spilling over her breasts.

"Then what is this?" he demanded.

"It's me showing you that I trust you," she snapped.

She looked away, wrapping her arms around her waist and taking a deep breath. Will paused, the anger burning out of him as what she said combined with her body language told him to pay attention.

"What do you mean?" he asked softly, having to consciously hold himself back from touching her.

She glanced back at him, searching his face for a heartbeat. Then she dropped her arms to her sides. "Those papers are about proving to you that you mean more to me than the ranch."

He shook his head. "How does it do that?"

"Well… I had Dad revise his will to give you the ranch if we don't stay married. And I'm giving it to you if we do. No kids involved."

Will swallowed. Hope rose inside him, greater than any he'd allowed himself since meeting his wife.

"What do you want?" he asked.

He needed her to take the last step to bring them together.

AT LEAST HE wasn't yelling at her anymore. When he'd come in here brandishing the papers, she'd had to work to keep her knees holding her up. She was already nervous as hell. She'd never put her heart out there like she was about to.

She licked suddenly dry lips. Her father was right, she'd never backed down from a fight in her life, and she wasn't backing down now. But that didn't make it any less terrifying. She had no idea which way things were about to go.

"I want you," she said. Simple as that.

Will put his hands on his hips, dropping his head to stare at the ground for a long moment. Rusty's heart pounded against her ribs as she waited.

He raised his eyes, pinning her with an intense blue gaze that made her stomach flutter.

"You want to stay married to me?" he asked.

She nodded. He took a step closer.

"For real?"

Another nod. Another step.

"Forever?"

"Yes," she whispered.

He stopped close enough that she could feel the heat of

his body.

"Why?" he asked.

And suddenly she saw it. A vulnerability underneath the quiet, confident cowboy he showed the world.

Please.

She did the only thing she could. She closed the small distance between them, pressing into him, and took his face in her hands. "Because I love you."

He didn't say anything at first, but she could feel his heart beating against her.

When he didn't speak, she hiked up her bravery and kept going. "I love you, Williams Hill. I think I've loved you since the first time you kissed me, even though I didn't want to admit it."

His blue eyes softened, and he slid his hands up her arms to circle her wrists with his hands, holding her touch to him, not letting her pull away. "Keep going," he murmured. "You're doing fine."

A bubble of elation came out as a hiccupping giggle. The words she'd been holding back for months poured from her. "You are the best man I've ever met. I know trust is difficult for me, but you can teach me. I know you can. I don't want the ranch or any other dreams I've spun if I can't share them with you."

He pulled her hands from his face.

Oh God. He was going to reject her.

But before the tears stinging the backs of her eyes could

spill over, he dropped his head to kiss the palms of both her hands.

Then looked back up, a smile lightening those blue eyes. "I love you, too," he said, his voice deeper, rougher than usual.

"You do?" she squeaked.

He nodded, a smile coming from some place deep and happy. "With everything I have in me. You busted into my life, and I feel like I've been holding on for my eight seconds ever since."

Rusty launched herself into his arms, laughing and crying at the same time, needing to hold him and be held. "I'm sorry about earlier today," she whispered.

He pulled back and smoothed her hair out of her face. "What made you realize I would never work against you that way?"

She shook her head. "I knew it even as I said it. I was just so mad at Dad. He says he's sorry, by the way, for almost messing this up."

Will raised his eyebrows. "I'd love to hear more about that, but not right now."

"Oh?"

He took her by the hand and tugged her out of the room, waving to the lady behind the desk who she'd convinced to help her and who glowed back, then pulled her up the stairs.

"Nope. I think we need a honeymoon and we're going to

start right now."

A happy giggle escaped her. "I finally wear a dress and—"

"And I can't wait to take it off you."

They made it to his door which he unlocked, but before she could move inside, he swung her up into his arms. "The groom carries the bride across the threshold."

She snuggled into him.

"Is the blue color for me?"

She nodded. "It reminds me of your eyes. I think blue might replace pink in my wardrobe moving forward."

He smiled at her, and her heart, already floating, soared.

He walked into the room, kicking the door closed behind him. With a slow deliberation, Will undressed them both before laying her down on the bed. He took his time, worshiping every inch of her and driving her need higher and higher with each kiss, each touch. And now, in each of those caresses, she could feel his love.

Rusty's heart wanted to fly away at the look in Will's eyes. Even giving as much as he had, she could see now he'd still held a part of himself back. Until this moment. Now she had all of Will.

She opened her own heart, vowing to give him all of herself in return. Every part of her.

After they reached heaven together, he pulled the blankets up over them, tucking her tenderly into his side, even as he pushed up on one elbow to stare down at her as though he was a little afraid she'd disappear.

But she never would. "I love you," she whispered.

He smiled, tucking a strand of her hair behind her ear. "I love you too, but I have one condition, Mrs. Hill," he said in that low, sexy rasp.

"Oh?" She smiled and raised her eyebrows in question, not remotely worried about what this mysterious condition might be. A little eager, in fact, to hear it.

Will went all serious and intense. "Marry me."

Despite the bubbles of exultation fluttering through her, she still couldn't help but tease. "We're already married," she pointed out.

"No. I mean, I want a church ceremony, with you in that gorgeous frilly dress and all of our family there. Marry me, again. For real this time."

Rusty gave a happy sigh, snuggling into him. "I'd love to."

Epilogue

RUSTY CHECKED HER dress one more time, and adjusted her grip on the bouquet, the sweet scent of the flowers wafting around her. She'd been here before, only this time the flutters in her tummy weren't dread or worry, but excitement and total confidence. This time her marriage vows meant something completely different.

The entire occasion felt different.

She glanced at Carter and a very pregnant Holly, who twinkled back at her. Somewhere in the chapel, Carter's new fiancé sat with the rest of the extended family. Sophia, in her adorable pink flower girl dress, was already on her way down the aisle, her blond ringlets bouncing with each step.

Rusty's father couldn't walk her down the aisle this time—already seated at the front with Evaline and John. The chemo had taken its toll, leaving him weak, frail. She'd once thought him invincible, but the body had a sad way of proving that wrong, even for the strongest. But he was here to see her married—really married, and to a man she loved more than she could put into words.

His tactics may have been on the hard side, but she had

to give her father credit. She wouldn't be here without his doing what he'd done. And she wouldn't be who she was without him either. In the last few months, they'd spent more time together, even just a week or two at a time, than they had in years. Forgiveness was a powerful healer.

Carter and Holly took their places at the front, with Will's brothers lined up beside him. The music changed and now it was her turn. The congregation rose and turned, smiles beaming at her as Rusty walked herself down the red-carpeted aisle.

They'd debated having someone else stand in for her father. But in the end, she'd decided that no one could replace Garrett Walker…or who he'd made her into. A strong, independent woman who could damn well give herself away.

The soft material of her dress—the same gorgeous pale pink and white gown she'd worn the first time—floated around her. Everything slowed and quieted as her gaze landed on Will. Breath-stealing handsome in a black tux, he stood very still watching her with those blue eyes and her heart took off, soaring. According to Will, she'd been his ever since he'd caught her dancing and singing in her truck at a stoplight in Estes Park, Colorado. But now…even after months of whispered I love yous, and falling asleep in his arms at night, and waking to his smile in the mornings…now this felt real.

The small chapel in town—quaint with the white wood siding and old-fashioned steeple on top, all dark hardwoods on the inside, beautifully carved—was filled with all their friends and family. Admittedly more folks on Will's side this time, which was as it should be. The man had a huge family when you added in all the aunts and uncles and cousins. Plus, it seemed that the entire town of La Colinas, and most of the surrounding ranches had shown.

Doris and Evaline both sniffled, especially when Rusty paused at her father's wheelchair and leaned down to kiss him on a papery cheek. Even the indomitable Garrett Walker's eyes glistened as she pulled away. "Thank you, Dad," she whispered.

He would know she was thanking him for who she was and where she was now—despite the rough road to get here. He squeezed her hand, and Rusty knew that meant he loved her. Even if he never said the words.

With a deep breath, she turned to her husband, to the man who'd never given up on her, proving by every look, every word, every action how much he loved her.

He held out his hand. "Are you ready, Mrs. Hill?"

Rusty cocked her head, though she couldn't contain her smile as she put her hand in his. "I think I've been ready since a cowboy tipped his imaginary hat at me when he caught me singing in my truck. I just didn't know it then."

Will's slow smile was everything she could have ever asked for. He drew her hand through his arm…and she was home.

The End

The Hills of Texas

For the Hills of Texas, ranching is a legacy, hard work is a way of life, and having siblings is like having a best friend you can't get rid of. You know whatever you do, they'll still be there. Family will stand by you, stand with you, stand behind you, and sometimes give you that needed push. Especially when it comes to finding love.

Book 1: *Saving the Sheriff*

Book 2: *Resisting the Rancher*

Book 3: Coming soon

Available now at your favorite online retailer!

About the Author

Award-winning contemporary romance author, Kadie Scott, grew up consuming books and exploring the world through her writing. She attempted to find a practical career related to her favorite pastime by earning a degree in English Rhetoric (Technical Writing). However, she swiftly discovered that writing without imagination is not nearly as fun as writing with it.

No matter the genre, she loves to write witty, feisty heroines, sexy heroes who deserve them, and a cast of lovable characters to surround them (and maybe get their own stories). She currently resides in Austin, Texas, with her own personal hero, her husband, and their two children, who are growing up way too fast.

Kadie also writes award-winning paranormal romance under the name Abigail Owen.

Thank you for reading

Resisting the Rancher

If you enjoyed this book, you can find more from all our great authors at TulePublishing.com, or from your favorite online retailer.

Made in the USA
Middletown, DE
28 July 2022